# Skeleton Hand

It wasn't aces and eights – the so-called dead man's hand – that the skeleton was holding, but he was definitely dead.

Cut loose by the Domino Ranch, Cody Hawk and his friends are facing a winter without work. So when the cowboys come across the skeleton it leads them to its treasure of gold and yet right into a deadly game, up against a band of killers and a money-hungry woman.

As they make their way across the empty land it seems that the skeleton isn't holding the only deadly hand: Cody Hawk will need the luck of the draw, and some help from a wild mountain girl, to survive. . . .

# Skeleton Hand

C.J. Sommers

A Black Horse Western

ROBERT HALE · LONDON

ISBN 978-0-7198-0991-0

Robert Hale Limited
Clerkenwell House
Clerkenwell Green
London EC1R 0HT

www.halebooks.com

*To Owen Irons,*
*friend and mentor*

Typeset by
Derek Doyle & Associates, Shaw Heath
Printed and bound in Great Britain by
CPI Antony Rowe, Chippenham and Eastbourne

# ONE

The cold rain slanted down through the moisture-heavy dark pines. Wraiths of cloud wove their way across the mountain top. The weary horses plodded on through the damp and cold and dark of the night. The three men mounted on them bowed their heads in surrender to the rain and the wind gusts and to the exhaustion that had settled upon them after hours in the saddle.

Lightning crackled, illuminating the huge pines and their trembling upper reaches, where boughs clacked against each other as the pursuing wind drove ferociously against the forest as if it were trying its best to knock the ancient trees down. Now and then a branch would crack and break free and fly past as if being aimed at them by the storm spirits. Thunder rumbled as the lightning flickered out and the riders of the forest had to halt their horses while their eyes readjusted to the darkness and surveyed the land as best they could under these conditions.

The roll and thrust of the mountain was a dark

puzzle to trail-weary, night-blind eyes. The three men were only specters to each other as the rain fell in a swamping torrent. The gray, cold fingers of the low clouds teased them and sank their heavy damp fingers into their bones.

Therefore, it was something of a miracle to them when they found themselves abruptly in a clearing stippled with broken, mossy stumps, and saw the poor shack standing there, bowed and huddled among the vast pine forest, squatting beneath the fury of the storm, rain streaming from its slanted roof.

'Look!' Wayne Tucker shouted, but his voice could hardly be heard among the slap and wash of the storm. Besides, his trail mates had seen the shack with its promise of shelter before he had spoken. They guided their weary horses nearer and swung down from their saddles as a gust of wind brought a wash of heavy downpour over them, blotting out all vision.

Charlie Tuttle had stepped up onto what remained of a low, sagging porch to try his shoulder against the door. 'Got it!' Charlie said with triumph. They watched as he nudged the door open on its flimsy leather hinges and entered the darkness of the shack. There was a dilapidated awning hanging crookedly from the face of the shack with a few boards missing from it. Wayne Tucker and Cody Hawk stood in its slight shelter, arms folded, heads bowed. Shivering and half-frozen, they waited as patiently as dumb animals until, miraculously, a feeble light flared up inside the cabin and a minute later Charlie Tuttle reappeared, shielding a flickering candle with his cupped hand.

'Come on inside, boys,' Charlie said. 'Haven't you got enough sense to get out of the rain?'

They didn't wait for a second invitation. The wind slapped at their backs, nearly propelling them into the shack, as if the storm had had enough of them. The feeble candle illuminated very little. Charlie had placed it in its tin boat on the mantel of the stone fireplace. It guttered in the draft of the wind until Cody managed to worry the flimsy door closed again.

By the faint yellow glimmer of the candle, Cody was able to see that the shack was nothing but a thrown-together structure of poles and pine bark with corner timbers. Mud had been used for caulking, and through chinks in this rough material the cold wind continued to make its way easily. It was the sort of place a man would throw up as a temporary structure over a winter, perhaps two, but which no one would willingly occupy for long.

'A trapper's cabin,' Charlie said as if he had been thinking along with Cody. 'A place for a man to hide out from the elements while trying to take thick winter pelts.'

'One winter in and then gone,' Wayne Tucker, who was still shuddering, agreed. 'When the winter pelts were gone, so was the trapper.'

'He took some time building that stone fireplace and the chimney,' Cody said.

The two older men stared at him.

'Well, he'd have to, wouldn't he? You ever spent a winter in an Indian hogan where all they have is a smoke hole and the wind shoves all the smoke right back in? No, he had to have a chimney if nothing else, to winter up here.'

'Bless him for it,' Charlie said. 'Now what do you say we try putting it to use? Find some wood, men.'

'I don't see any stacked around,' Wayne Tucker answered snappishly. 'Why don't you go out and chop down a tree, Charlie?'

'The wood would be green,' Charlie said. 'Why don't you do it yourself? Or go suck eggs – it don't matter to me.'

'We can maybe use some of the bark he has tacked up on the walls,' Cody said. His two trail mates seemed ready to descend into one of their endless, bickering fights.

'Sure,' Charlie said with mockery. 'Let's start burning the whole place down piece by piece until we end up standing out in the storm in front of a nice warm fire.'

'I was just thinking,' Cody said, with a note of apology. 'That bark isn't doing anything to cut the wind now.' He walked to the near wall and fingered the slabs of pine bark attached to it. These were dry and would come off easily. 'It would be something, at least.'

'There's a bedframe in this corner,' Charlie Tuttle said. 'We could sacrifice it, too, I suppose. And there's that crummy little table and two chairs.'

'The trapper wouldn't like it a bit if he returns to find his place ruined,' Wayne Tucker commented.

Charlie laughed at the remark. 'Look around the place, Wayne! Smell it. Nothing but damp rot and animal scent. Dust inches thick. Whoever threw this shack up is gone and has been gone for years. He's had enough; he won't be back to winter up here again.'

Wayne only grunted his answer. Cody, poking around in the dimness for something else to burn, had found a stack of pelts in one corner. Stiff as boards, they were, and the value of the furs had been destroyed by the depredations of rodents. Why hadn't the trapper packed these away while they were still prime? Maybe the man had wandered out on some winter night and never made it back.

'Did you find anything to eat?' Charlie asked Wayne, who had located a small cupboard near the table.

'Just a few sirloin steaks and mashed potatoes. Why don't you go out and milk the cow so we'll have something to drink with it?'

Charlie swallowed a hostile reply. Or maybe he just couldn't come up with anything snappy enough. 'Come on, kid, your idea about taking some of this bark down wasn't half bad. It's not doing anything to keep the weather out.'

Maybe the primitive insulation had once done what it was intended to do, but time and the constant onslaught of the rainstorm had rendered it useless. Charlie Tuttle gripped a section of pine bark with both hands and tore it free of its wall mounts. Cody set to removing another panel. Powdered bark and dust showered down on him as he pulled the slab free. Charlie, on his knees at the hearth, was chopping at the bark with his big Bowie knife, cutting it into useable lengths. The candlelight flickered across his intent face.

9

By that wavering light, the usually affable Charlie Tuttle appeared a little demonic. His small mouth was tightly puckered, his thin dark hair fell across his forehead. He cursed as a piece of wood shifted unexpectedly and he caught a long splinter in the heel of his hand. His round face was incredibly intent. Cody realized that he was watching a man who was fighting for survival. It really hadn't come home to Cody Hawk that they were in a life-threatening situation until then. In the high-up mountains the outside temperature could plummet thirty or forty degrees before morning. He had been cold all afternoon, but it was nothing like it would be overnight. If they had not stumbled across this shack, they likely would not have survived to see the sun rise.

Probably this explained the tension between Charlie and Wayne.

'Hold it!' Wayne shouted and Cody left off prying at another section of bark. But it was Charlie Tuttle whom Wayne was yelling at. Charlie had broken off some dry chunks of bark and was now rubbing them between his calloused hands to make tinder of them. A small cone of similar material sat in the hearth, ready to be lit.

'That chimney might be blocked up, Charlie. You know what owls and varmints will do to a chimney over years of neglect. Raccoons use them for a den, raising a whole litter of baby 'coons in them once they come to think it's a safe, protected place. Owls will clog the whole thing up with nesting. . . .'

Charlie had taken enough. He got to his feet and stood facing his friend. 'I was going to have my look before I started a fire, Wayne!'

'You sure didn't look like it,' Wayne snapped back.

'Well, I was,' Charlie said defiantly. Now it was Wayne's craggy, mustached face that showed plainly in the poor light of the candle. He was biting at his lower lip, his disgust a fixed expression.

'You never take the time to think things out before you do them,' Wayne grumbled.

'And you never do nothing!' Charlie barked back.

The two continued to glare at each other. They had always been that way. As long as Cody Hawk had known them, and that was going on three years now. Cody, they generally left alone. They still considered him a kid, and deserving of or needing nothing more than quiet scoldings, whereas the two he-bears were sometimes ready to start growling at each other over the most trivial things.

Cody watched them eyeing each other, nearly nose to nose. It wouldn't last long; then they would find a new point of contention. Cody supposed he was just used to them; it didn't bother him any more. He was like a kid who had been brought up in a house where complaints and arguments were the norm.

A *kid*. Sometimes Cody bristled at being referred to that way. He had been walking around this planet for nearly a quarter of a century now and had branded, roped and pushed cattle with Wayne and Charlie for over three years back on the Domino. Cody smiled as he pried another piece of bark away from the wall. In a way both of the men – Charlie and Wayne – considered him to be their younger brother, and in a way it was a

11

comfort to him. It was, Cody decided, only because he still had a full crop of curly hair and a flat belly that they considered him to be a kid.

Turning, Cody placed the slab of bark near the fireplace. Charlie was looking up the chimney with the aid of the candle while Wayne scowled. A massive gust of wind hit the cabin; a wall of northern air shook the flimsy structure to its unsubstantial foundations.

It would snow. Cody knew that as sure as he knew his own name and it added immediacy to his movements. They were not going to freeze to death here in this shabby cabin on the mountain if Cody could help it.

He considered knocking the furniture apart, but the bark was easier to come by and besides they might welcome the small, primitive comfort of having a chair to sit down and rest on after they had built their fire.

Working his way along the front wall, pulling down the bark facing, he came to the pile of stiff, ruined pelts and toed them aside. Something moved beneath them. Cody stepped back and swallowed hard.

Charlie had chinned himself on a ledge inside the chimney. Now he lowered himself again. His hands and face were black with soot, his round face resembling an unhappy minstrel's.

'I can't see the sky,' Charlie puffed.

'What did I tell you?' Wayne answered as if his point had been made.

Charlie bristled but did not react. 'Something's blocking it up,' he answered. 'Give me that fireplace poker there. I might be able to clear it.'

Wayne handed Charlie the tool and squatted on his

heels, watching and waiting as Charlie Tuttle half-disappeared up the chimney, grumbling as he went. Soot floated down, blackening the floor around the fireplace. Wayne sleeved the ash from his face and waited expectantly. He was shivering again and wanted a fire built more than he would admit to the others. Wayne prided himself on his toughness, but the rising storm and falling temperature were enough to smother false pride.

'Anything?' Wayne yelled with a touch of anxiety. He sat rocked back on his heels, his arms clasped around his body. Another explosive burst of thunder shook the shack with a following blast of cold wind. The cabin trembled violently and Wayne Tucker began to think the flimsy hut could not withstand this winter storm. Cody Hawk stood in the corner, unmoving, his expression one of fixed fear – what was wrong with the kid?

'I've got it hooked!' Charlie called down the chimney, his voice echoing from the close confines.

'What is it – an owl's nest?'

'Hold on . . . I've almost got it loose!'

They heard Charlie grunt with effort, curse, and then he fell from the chimney in a shower of soot and debris. Charlie hit the flooring roughly and sat, rubbing his shoulder, his face, hands and clothing as black as a dirty night. In his lap was the object.

'What in the hell is that?' Wayne Tucker asked.

'It's what was causing all the trouble,' Charlie said, still rubbing his injured shoulder.

Wayne moved nearer and waved the candle over the item. What it was, Wayne realized, was a pair of battered,

13

time-rotted saddle-bags.

'Now what kind of fool trick. . . ?' Wayne muttered, taking the saddle-bags from Charlie's legs and placing them on the floor beside him. 'Who shoves his saddle-bags up a chimney?' The leather bags, he had noticed, were heavier than they had the right to be. They might have been filled with stones.

He had already opened one of the bags, finding the straps stiff and rotted.

'My God, boys!' Wayne said as Charlie dragged himself out of the fireplace and to his feet. 'We've found a hidden treasure.'

'What are you talking about?' Charlie asked, his voice a growl.

'Have a look, Charlie!' Wayne crowed. 'Tell me you don't see gold, minted gold, inside the bag. Open up the other side – it's a fortune, boys! I'm telling you someone left a fortune in gold hidden away in the chimney.'

'Where would a fur trapper come by that kind of money?' Charlie asked, rubbing his arm still.

'We don't know that it was the trapper. It could have been anyone passing through who needed a place to sit out a storm – some bank robber on the run, maybe,' Wayne told him, looking up from the saddle-bags, a handful of gold coins nestled in his palm.

'That makes sense – I guess,' Charlie answered. 'If so, you can bet he'll be coming back to retrieve this.' Charlie's eyes flickered toward the door.

'In this weather?' Wayne laughed mockingly. 'Besides, these saddle-bags are old, very old. Whatever happened here happened a long time ago. Look at the dates on these gold pieces! Not a single one was coined less than fifteen years ago. Probably,' Wayne went on to speculate, 'whoever hid them – some thief – went on his way and had an accident along the trail. Maybe he got himself caught for some other crime and they hung him.'

'Maybe he didn't. Maybe he's going to be coming back at any time,' Charlie said dubiously.

Cody hadn't spoken for a time. He hadn't been able to. His throat was tight, dry and useless for speech. Now he did speak.

'I don't think he'll be coming back,' Cody said. 'I don't think he ever left. Either that, or he left his hand behind.'

As the two older men went to where Cody Hawk stood, he again toed the pile of stiff ancient pelts lying in the corner of the wind-blown cabin. He moved the hides just enough to reveal the fleshless bony hand concealed beneath them.

# TWO

The firelight produced by the burning of the rotting, beetle-infested bark sent a bright glow if little warmth around the interior of the trapper's shack where Charlie, Wayne and Cody Hawk sat around the bare plank table. There were eight stacks of gold coins sitting on the table top, and these shimmered brightly. Now and then a flare-up of flame also crossed the ivory fingers of the skeleton in the corner. The expressions of the men were variously glum, cheerful and concerned. None of them had ever found himself in a predicament quite like this. It would take some studying on.

'Three thousand, eight hundred dollars,' said Wayne, who had assumed the role of banker.

'Where it came from is what I want to know,' Charlie, who carried the most gloom, said. He stood near the fire, which he considered his personal triumph. His face was still dark with soot, his eyes dim with misery. Now and then Cody would notice the round man glance toward the cabin door as the wind and rain caused some part of the old shack to rattle or moan. Just then an especially strong gust of buffeting wind caused the shack to shimmy and seem to threaten to collapse around them.

'That man over there,' Wayne said, flagging a thumb across his shoulder in the direction of the skeleton, 'must have been the thief. He knew he was dying and had time to hide the loot in the chimney where he thought no one would ever find it.'

'Maybe,' was what Charlie responded.

That seemed to infuriate Wayne. 'Well, what else could it be!'

Cody pushed away from the table and rose. Wayne, he knew, was just trying to provoke one of the pair's constant squabbles. These were usually pointless and led nowhere; Cody had learned to take no part in their heated discussions, which he had seen descend into such small disputes as to the merits of homemade fish hooks and whether a man could get fleas in his mustache. Cody walked toward the hand seeming to reach out from under the hides in a silent plea.

'I think the dead man,' Charlie said after a long period of meditation during which he studied the wavering flames in the fireplace, 'somehow got hold of another man's money and that he was tracked down, threatened, tortured and killed when he wouldn't give it up.'

'Pretty much what I was saying,' Wayne commented.

'No, it isn't, Wayne,' Charlie argued. 'I'm saying he was murdered by another man – and that one might just come back looking for the gold. If he finds us . . .'

17

'I can take care of any man that comes looking,' Wayne said with assurance. He leaned back in the puncheon chair, hooking his thumbs behind his gunbelt.

'Maybe there's more than one man,' Charlie pointed out. 'It's a big haul wherever it came from. There was probably more than one man in on the job.' He added nervously, 'I'm saying maybe we shouldn't be hanging around here. We've got the loot – let's go.'

'In that storm? On this night? We wouldn't make it off this mountain alive, Charlie.'

'I'm more worried now about making it out of this cabin alive.'

From the corner where the dead man lay, Cody Hawk asked them, 'What do you think this could mean?'

'What?' Wayne answered with irritation. He was just working himself up to a new line of argument and didn't like to be interrupted when he was ready to launch one of his scathing salvos.

'Come over and take a look,' Cody said. He was squatting on his heels beside the skeleton, which he had now fully uncovered. Wayne and Charlie shuffled that way. 'Look at that,' Cody said, pointing something out. By the feeble, shifting firelight Wayne and Charlie could make out what the kid was talking about.

The skeleton's other hand, previously concealed, held a group of pasteboard cards. Charlie felt a shiver go up his spine as he crouched down to take a look. Was the skeleton still holding its own cards – a true dead man's hand?

'There's five of them,' Cody pointed out. 'A poker hand?'

18

Unceremoniously Wayne Tucker leaned over and slipped away the playing cards, which had been thrust between the dead man's first two fingers and not where they would have been if they had been gripped by his thumb.

The cards were cracked, bent and falling apart. Wayne studied them with a frown of concentration. 'Ten,' he announced, studying the cards, 'eight, seven, six, jack.'

'And?' asked Cody, who had never acquired skill with or any interest in card-playing.

'Good bluffing hand,' Charlie said thoughtfully, 'if the game was five-card stud and whoever he was betting against thought our friend here had a nine to go with the other cards and not the wild jack. The other man might have thought this one was holding a straight—'

'He could have won a pot if he was a good enough bluffer,' Wayne added for Cody's education. 'The jack busted his hand, but his opponent could have believed that he had a nine, filling the straight. Money has been lost on less.'

'But why leave those cards in his hand like this?' Cody wondered.

'Maybe someone flipped his cards over and found the jack instead of the nine, got mad as hell at himself for losing a pot to a broken straight and went away, coming back later to take his revenge.'

'After the skeleton – whoever he was – had gotten worried and hidden his take in the chimney,' Charlie contributed.

'Would someone. . . ?' Cody asked.

19

'For almost four thousand dollars?' Wayne answered. 'You bet, Cody. I think that's what happened here – why else leave that hand of cards in the dead man's fingers?'

'I'm afraid you're right,' Charlie said glumly, agreeing with his partner for once. Firelight painted his face red and soot-black. His concern was evident. Cody covered the skeleton once more and the three men stood in a tight circle, discussing matters as the storm battered the ramshackle cabin.

'I don't know who might have done the killing, or how long ago it was,' Charlie said, almost stuttering as he spoke. 'But I'm for getting out of here as quickly as we can.'

Now it was time for the argumentative Wayne Tucker to agree. 'Just as soon as this storm blows itself out, we're leaving.'

Cody was still unsure of how this could have happened – losing almost $4,000 in a card game in an isolated shack.

Charlie enlightened him. 'You see, kid, this man – I guess we have to assume he was a thief – maybe got caught in a storm like this one. Maybe it was dark and he couldn't find his way. He stumbles across the shack like we did, and the man over there,' he said, nodding toward the pile of skins, 'grateful for any company in this wilderness, invited him in.

'Say the storm holds for days, or maybe the thief has some sort of injury that keeps him from traveling on immediately – it doesn't matter which – but he gets bored and suggests a friendly card game.'

20

'How could this man, the trapper, have enough money to gamble against the wealthy thief?' Cody asked.

Wayne spoke up: 'Easy. Say the trapper, an old man tight with a dollar out of necessity, had ten or twenty dollars stuck away in a sock: survival money. He could play for that if he were so inclined.'

'Sure,' Charlie agreed. 'The thief just wanted to pass the time anyway. Gambling can be a strange or even humbling experience. I can see the trapper turning ten dollars into twenty, twenty into fifty. . . .'

'He falls into a lucky streak,' Wayne said. 'Maybe the thief let him win the early hands, who knows? Soon they're sitting at this table in front of the fire while the storm whips and slashes at the shack. Maybe there's snow drifted up around the place. The thief knows he's gotten in too deep, but he keeps on playing cards. There's sweat glistening on his brow now as he frets. Maybe the last hand comes down to all that has passed across the table, and the expressionless trapper is holding – well, we know what cards he was holding, don't we?'

'Six, seven, eight and ten,' Cody said, remembering.

'Right,' Charlie said. 'Then the last card is dealt, face down, and the expressionless trapper starts raising the pot and the thief has to follow.'

'While he starts to believe by the size of the raise that the trapper has drawn the nine he needed for that straight.'

'The thief starts to understand what a fool he has been, throws down his cards and demands to see the trapper's last card.'

'He flips it over and that one-eyed jack is staring at him,' Wayne said with a sort of muted glee, as if he had been cheering for the old trapper all the while.

'The trapper rakes in the gold, with thanks, while the thief blusters away about being bluffed, cheated. He had put a lot of devilish work into gathering that money – whether it came from a bank or some freight office, whatever, and he wasn't ready to give it up to an old fool in some forlorn shack. Especially not over a bluff.'

'He was like most gamblers who shouldn't be at card tables,' Wayne agreed. 'He took the chance and lost and should have never sat to the table if he couldn't stand the loss.'

'He probably never took that into consideration, seeing where he was and who he was playing against. He seems to have been a violent man anyway – he took the only solution that offered itself.'

'He went out, maybe rode for a time until he got to festering and knew he had to come back and kill the trapper, who by then had decided to take no chances and stuffed the gold up the chimney,' Wayne said.

Charlie guessed, 'The thief must have swatted the trapper around, maybe tortured him, crazy to recover the money, but the trapper wouldn't surrender it – he must have had ideas about chucking this rough wilderness life for the comfort of a soft, familiar bed every night. But there was no stopping the enraged bandit, and when he knew he wasn't going to get any more out of the trapper, he killed him. Then he probably tore

22

the place apart, his wildness growing as his frustration built upon itself.'

'It makes a good story,' Cody said, 'but we don't know if any of it is true.'

'No?' Charlie asked, his round face somber. 'Then give us another idea as to why a concealed skeleton would have those pasteboards shoved in his dead hand. It was fury that caused that final gesture.'

'I suppose you're right,' Cody answered, again unwilling to get into any debate with either of his two companions. Did he believe the story? He wasn't sure. There was a kind of logic to it, of course, but they would never know the truth of things and Cody, for his part, was not sure he would ever want to. Right now he was only interested in sleeping and passing the night in relative comfort while the furious storm continued to blow across the mountain slopes. The two older men seated themselves again at the puncheon table where stacks of gold still glittered coldly in the hearth-light.

'I'm turning in, boys,' Cody said, snatching up his bedroll. 'Who's got the bed?' He nodded toward the wood-frame bed the trapper had built for his own use. Charlie and Wayne revealed their avuncular side as they answered almost as one:

'Take it, kid.' Charlie told him, 'I've been too long in the rough to even remember what a mattress feels like.'

'You're younger,' Wayne added, his hatchet-sharp face clear in the glowing embers of the dying fire. Smoke trickled down across the hearth, evidence that rising smoke was being defeated by the blustering wind

23

outside the shack. 'You need your rest. Take the bed; we won't disturb you unless we decide we have to start burning the furniture to keep warm.'

Cody nodded thankfully and rolled out his blankets on the thin tick mattress, which smelled of mildew and age. No matter, he was warm and comfortable enough. The last thing he heard anyone say before he went off to sleep was Wayne suggesting:

'Want to play a game of cards, Charlie?'

Morning was bright, crisp but untroubled by the storm clouds. The long ranks of pine stood straight and blue along the flanks of the mountains, their boughs frosted with the snow that had come in the night. Cody Hawk stood on the dilapidated porch of the shack for a moment, breathing in the cold clean air, then he walked across the new-fallen snow toward the miserable horses, which had been forced to spend the intolerable night in the open. He approached his own buckskin horse apologetically, noting that the animal's whiskers and eyelashes were still sheathed in ice.

'Sorry, Buck,' Cody said, running his gloved hand along the horse's flank. 'It just couldn't be helped.'

Blue jays flitted among the frozen pines and sunlight glittered across the snowfields. The wind gusted and swayed the trees, shaking snow loose from their upper boughs, but it was neither a hard nor a constant wind. Cody whisked the flecks of ice and snow from his horse's back and slipped the reluctant animal its bit before he smoothed the blanket and threw his saddle up, feeling no more eager to be moving on this chilly morning than the buckskin did.

Charlie Tuttle, bundled in his sheepskin coat, appeared on the porch, studying the cold skies. Then, slapping his gloved hands together he approached his own roan horse. A look of pity came over Charlie's round, ruddy face and he stroked the sleek animal's neck in apology.

'I feel sorry for the beasts. The only way it could have been worse,' he said to Cody, 'was if it had been us stuck out here overnight. Unsettling as it was spending the night with a dead man, I still give thanks for that trapper's shack.'

Wayne Tucker was the last to appear. He stood on the porch squinting into the bright winter sunlight, his saddle-bags slung over his shoulder. They looked quite heavy now.

'He transferred the gold coin to his own bags and burned the old ones,' Charlie said, although Cody could have guessed that. What smoke there was seeping up into the unsettled sky smelled faintly of burning leather. And Wayne looked quite pleased with himself, the shadow of a smile appearing across his craggy face beneath his drooping mustache.

He strapped the heavy saddle-bags behind his saddle and together the three continued on their journey. The storm had blown them off their course along the Long Cut, the only way over the mountains, but now they were able to find the traveled path again and continue through the cool of morning.

'Don't like having that dead man's gold with us,' Charlie muttered as he rode close to Cody Hawk.

'It made no sense to leave it,' Cody said, looking up at the blue sky above the trembling pines. 'What would you have had him do?'

'I just don't like toting it, that's all,' Charlie snapped back defensively. 'It don't spook me that it belonged to a dead man, but whoever killed him hasn't forgotten. He's remembered that gold he thinks he was cheated out of for long years – and if he were to know we had found it, he'd come to take it back.'

'How would he know?' Cody asked. 'None of us is going to say a word, that's for sure.'

'Maybe he'll just keep watching,' Charlie went on. 'This is the only trail out of the mountains. Maybe he sits watching for day after day, waiting for his gold.'

'That's insane talk, Charlie. Nobody would do a thing like that – after the years have passed.'

'No one but a crazy man. You're right, Cody, it is insane talk, and we might have an insane man to deal with.'

Cody quit listening. Charlie's imagination was running away with him. The thief, whoever he was, might have been a little crazy, but no one was insane enough to spend years sitting and watching this rugged trail. Probably, Cody thought, Charlie was only scared – frightened of what this new-found wealth might bring.

Cody himself found that he honestly did not care about the fortune. Maybe because he was still young and had miles to travel, years to live. The two older men might have more need of the money. Enough wealth to buy themselves a small place where they could rest their joints, weary muscles worn down by the hard years of working cattle. A cowboy's life is not an easy one and it is a young man's work.

As Charlie had once said, 'It's work for a man too young to know what he's getting into.'

Cold camps, rough work, stampedes and hard winters took their toll over time.

Finally they reached the Rios Canyon, emerging from the deep pines to look down across the rugged land. Rios had been their goal from the first. Boss Allison, the foreman of the Domino ranch, had approached them in the bunkhouse three days ago, pointing them out and gathering them around him.

'Boys,' Allison had told them, 'round-up is long over and winter's about to set in. We can't afford to have a bunch of men sitting around here while it snows with nothing to do but pare their fingernails. I hope you'll understand.'

They did, but it didn't make it any more pleasant to take. Taking their packs, they had swung aboard their ponies and left the Domino, trying to make it through Long Cut before the snow began to fall.

There were other ranches down south, primarily the huge Triangle which, being lower in altitude, was a ranch that could work through most of the hard winters and, as many cowhands were nomads at heart, there was always a chance of finding jobs to fill.

The Triangle had been their goal from the start and still was.

Or so Cody Hawk thought.

The two older men seemed to be having different thoughts. When they paused at noon in an aspen grove the conversation between Charlie and Wayne turned to things they had never had, enjoyments they had never experienced and the possibility that they now had all of this within their grasp. Cody listened to their idle conversation as the wind ruffled the leaves of the golden aspens. Propped up on one elbow, chewing a bit of dry grass, he watched as the two older men became more animated, mentally counting the gold they now possessed.

'What's the matter with you?' Wayne demanded of Cody, noticing the faint disapproval on the kid's face. 'A cut of this money is yours, Cody. Isn't there anything you'd like to have?'

'Maybe something that comes in an expensive petticoat,' Charlie suggested jovially.

Cody grinned sheepishly and yawned. 'The truth is,' he told them, 'I'd be happy just to end up with what we started down here to get. A shelter for the winter and a good job waiting for me in the spring.'

'How many years of that do you want to go through?' Wayne said, again indicating the difference in their ages. 'Do you know how many bones I've had broken in my time on the range?'

'It's a rough life,' Charlie sympathized.

'I wouldn't know what to do with the money,' Cody said. 'I guess I could buy myself a little cottage outside of some town, and a rocking-chair for the front porch – then what would I do?'

'He's too young to know,' Charlie said, and Wayne nodded agreement. The buckskin horse wandered near Cody and nuzzled him, wondering when they were going to start traveling on. Cody stroked the horse's muzzle thoughtfully.

'I reckon I'll be all right, boys – no matter what you decide to do.'

Charlie stared at him; Wayne wagged his head as if in pity.

'There's this story I heard about money,' Cody said, rising to tighten the cinch straps on his saddle. 'It concerns a cowhand alone out on the long plains with little to eat and only a single blanket to keep him warm at nights. His only possessions his horse and a gun. He would sleep under the ice-cold stars, shivering and feeling that if he could only find some little cabin to shelter up in, he'd be the happiest man in the world.' Wayne and Charlie seemed to be listening intently.

'So, comes the day this cowboy found a small cabin to keep him from the cutting wind of the plains and the rains of winter. Well, he moved in and started slowly to build himself a herd of cattle on the land. The worries that go along with trying to protect it in that wilderness, to keep the predators away, the rustlers, wore on him, but he survived many cold winters and summer droughts, and in time found himself prosperous.

'He started to think he needed a fancier house, where he could welcome his friends and neighbors, one with bedrooms and a kitchen, nothing like his poor shack. It took him a while, but he built such a house. He was growing older now, of course. His herds increased and his power grew. So did his worries. At night, sleeping in his big soft bed, he would sometimes wonder what he had accomplished and wished for what had once been.

'He dreamed of being a lone cowboy out on the long prairie, sleeping under his poor blanket. It had been the best time of his life, you see.' Cody smiled and swung aboard his buckskin horse.

'Yeah, well,' Charlie said, 'I'll wager if the old man had gone out that night to try sleeping on the cold ground, his arthritis and rheumatism would have driven him back pretty quick to his warm bed.'

'I get it,' Wayne said, stepping into the saddle of his own horse. 'It's about a man never being satisfied with what he has, wanting more until he finds that it wasn't so much.'

'What about you, Wayne?' Charlie asked with a smile. 'Are you satisfied with what you have?'

'I am now, partner,' Wayne Tucker said, patting the gold-heavy saddle-bags behind his saddle. 'I am now.'

Cody Hawk shrugged and grinned. His point had been that he deserved to travel the rough road ahead of him and soak up its experiences. They were probably right – he was too young to know what kind of hell might lie ahead of him.

Transporting thousands of dollars in stolen gold was not going to make the road they traveled any easier.

# THREE

They rode down the Rios Canyon gorge, watching the cold, quick white water rushing through the gray walls of the gorge. There was a well-marked trail running along the bank so there was no need to concern themselves with trying to ford the frothing river, now churning with the recent rain and snowmelt. Cody doubted the river could be crossed anyway. It was cool in the canyon bottom, a brisk breeze whipping past. The three men rode hunched in their coats, shoulders nearly to their ears. There was an occasional small stand of pine trees and isolated cedars. Some new grass was trying to prosper, but not doing well. The weather was not conducive to the growth. They spotted a doe mule deer watering with her two half-grown fawns, but left them alone, although hunger was beginning to gnaw at them.

'Have you traveled this road before, Charlie?' Wayne asked, shouting to be heard above the swirl and roar of the rushing river.

'Once. The last time I got fired from a high country

ranch,' Charlie said with no apparent bitterness. 'I made my way to the Triangle that time too and got hired on. . . .'

'The reason I'm asking,' Wayne said, not in the mood for one of Charlie's long-winded tales, 'is that the traveling is going to get pretty rugged unless we find some graze for our ponies and some grub for ourselves. Is there any kind of stop over ahead? A town, maybe, a small ranch?'

'Not that I can recall,' Charlie answered. 'Of course the last time I was leading a pack-mule and didn't need to stop for anything.'

'You were so much smarter then,' Wayne said, just to chip in something abrasive. 'How about you, Cody?' Wayne asked. 'Have you ever ridden this way?'

'No, sir. I never even been on this side of the mountains in my life.'

Where had he been? Cody thought to himself. Nowhere, really, in his entire life. The Domino ranch had been his home for a long while. His idea of a town was McCormack, a shanty town thrown up mostly to take advantage of the high country ranches in the area. In McCormack a man could find liquor and gambling, and there were always a few tired-looking women trying to dress fancy but looking like they were only marking time until they reached the end of their trail. Cody found out early that he had no tolerance for liquor, no liking for gambling, and the women of the type he had met in McCormack held only an intimidating sort of fascination for him.

The riders had emerged from the mouth of the

gorge by noon, and the land fanned out around them in a long plain. There was not much green grass to be seen. The cold, driving rain the storm had delivered was not the nurturing sort.

With the sun high in the pale-blue sky they stopped to give their ponies a rest. There was nowhere to sit except on the muddy earth, so they just stood idly by and watched as their horses tried to forage a meal from what grass they could find.

'If we do find a farmhouse,' Charlie said, looking at the featureless land ahead, 'I say we offer the lady of the house good money for some country home cooking.'

'How much have you got in your purse, Charlie?' Wayne asked.

Charlie looked at the man in surprise, his red, round face set in a frown. 'Why, Wayne, we're carrying enough money to buy a farm and cook a chicken for ourselves.'

'No, we're not,' Wayne Tucker said with a harsh look that included Cody. 'We don't have that money. Understand? If we so much as flash one five-dollar gold piece, we'd better have our minds made up that we're willing to fight for it. There's plenty of thieves in this world, and we've still got a man wanting it back who figures it for his own.'

'The man who killed the trapper back there? Why, he must be long gone. It happened so long ago.'

'The killer will have a long, bitter memory of it. Maybe he thinks about it every morning when he rises and again before he rolls up for the night. He must have had a lot of dreams wrapped around that gold.'

'Ah, Wayne!' Charlie said in disgust. 'It's—'

'That's it, Charlie! Until we get somewhere where we can safely tuck that gold away, we show none of it. We don't even whisper about it. That's the only safe way.'

'All right,' Charlie said dourly. He knew that Wayne was right. He himself had seen a man killed for the boots he was wearing. There was a lot of poverty on the far plains, and a lot of rough men looking to remedy that.

They rode on into the afternoon, the lowering sun on their right shoulders. There was no trail and no need for any across the flat expanse. But that left them with little clue as to where they were going. Both men professed to know where the huge Triangle ranch lay, but there seemed to be no certainty in their direction.

By mid-afternoon they began to hear a new storm rumbling in the mountains they had just left and, looking that way, Cody saw black thunderheads stacked against the northern sky, shadowing the high country. It would storm again up there and probably the snow would fall heavily.

'Lucky we made it down,' Cody commented, 'before that settles in.'

'Probably would have froze to death,' Wayne said with a small shudder.

'Probably would have starved to death,' Charlie said in a complaining voice.

'We'll come across a place,' Wayne said.

'And do what? Stand looking at a pile of ham and sweet potatoes which we can afford to buy but don't

34

because you say that gold has got to stay hid? Why can't we chip a few dollars out of it?'

'It hasn't come up, has it, Charlie?' Wayne said, waving an arm around the empty land.

'You won't spend no money if it does!' Charlie said irritably. 'You already told us that.'

'Would you rather be hungry or dead?' Wayne asked angrily.

'It gets to the point where there's not much difference,' Charlie grumbled. Then he fell silent. Cody knew that it was just their habitual bickering, sharpened by the long miles in the saddle, the ordeal in the mountains and mounting hunger. If the two were not arguing they were not happy.

The wind continued to rise; the skies behind them grew darker. Now and then Cody would glance back northward, to measure the storm's progress. He did not wish to be caught out on the open prairie should the hard weather continue to approach. Once, as he shifted his eyes that way, Cody caught a glimpse of an unexpected sight.

He could not be sure in the tricky interweaving of light and shadow, it all being so distant, but he thought, believed, that if his eyes were not playing tricks on him, he had spotted a lone horseman following along their trail.

Cody said nothing about the horseman. It would lead to wild conjecture which would somehow become an argument between Charlie and Wayne. Anyway, he could not be positive. A man in lonesome country long enough starts to create familiar images in his mind where none exist. Still, Cody did not ride as easily as he previously had. For a single moment he had an unsettling, haunting thought:

*The skeleton wants its gold back.*

In the hour before sunset they began to see scattered cattle on the prairie.

Cody asked, 'Are we getting close to the Triangle?'

Charlie answered, 'No, we're another day's travel from Triangle. It looks like some boot-strapper is taking a gamble on the open range.'

Cody nodded. He understood what Charlie meant. Someone with nothing but a small herd of cattle and a lot of unjustified hope had apparently driven the animals onto unclaimed land. Cody had seen many men trying to make it like that. Sometimes it worked out for the new rancher; more often it was a desperate, ill-considered attempt that ended in tragedy for the rancher and his family.

'Maybe they've thrown up a ranch house,' Charlie said, his mind obviously still on his belly.

'Do you see anything?' Wayne asked, eager to maintain his sense of superiority. 'Probably it's a hole-in-the-ground outfit.'

Cody had seen some of those too. On the open plains where not a stick of timber grew, some shoestring ranchers had tried living there with nothing but a dugout hole in the ground as shelter. Covered over with brush as a roof and maybe some crude wattle, these brave, foolhardy types would sit out a winter in conditions as primitive as those endured by any nomadic tribe. Except the wandering Indian would already have ridden south, following the bison before heavy winter set in. People had been found, whole families, frozen or choked by smoke from fires which had only a hole in the roof to ventilate them. At times heavy snows would collapse the crude shelter, leaving those within with no protection from the weather, and no place for hundreds of miles to go.

Still men came and tried it. We are a resilient and a stubborn race.

They passed two red-backed cattle chewing away on their bovine cuds. These were neither contented with their lot nor disturbed at the prospect of a hard winter. It was doubtful they were able to understand either situation, and there was nothing they could do to change their fate. They were a useful, sad, enduring species.

'Those two have a little fat on them,' Charlie said, studying the cattle. 'Maybe we could cut one out. We could have us some beefsteak instead of swallowing our own dry spit for supper.' Charlie's eyes were fixed unhappily on Wayne. 'If anyone challenged us, we could offer to pay up.'

'When would you do that, Charlie?' Wayne growled. 'Before or after they fitted your neck in a noose?'

'Ah, everybody ain't that unreasonable!' Charlie complained.

He had more to add, but the sharp crack of a distant rifle and the slam of a well-aimed bullet brought the debate to a sudden end.

Cody had heard the bullet strike before he heard the report. The lead slug had whistled across the intervening space and whined off of the saddle-bags

Wayne's horse was carrying. The sound of the impact was like a muffled blacksmith's strike. The horse reared up in angry confusion; it had felt the impact of the bullet against its body and did not care for it even though it had caused no lasting harm.

Cody eased his own buckskin horse forward and grabbed the bridle of Wayne's horse. Nearly unseated by the rearing horse, Wayne was clinging to the dancing animal with the saddle pommel and a hand grasping the horse's mane.

Now Charlie had drawn his rifle from its sheath and was looking westward toward where the shot had originated. Cody saw nothing, no one. And then he did. Four armed men were walking toward them, only small shadows in the distance. They must have been hidden in some coulee that cut the land.

Or had they risen from their underground shelter?

Cody released his grip on the bridle of Wayne's horse as it settled, shaking its head in annoyance. He drew his own revolver and rested it on his lap, his hand firmly on the butt.

'Just hold up there!' a voice called in a distant, angry shout. 'We can pick you off those ponies one by one.'

'Why would you want to do that?' Charlie bellowed out in answer before realizing he did not want to get into a shouting match. More quietly he said to Cody, 'Don't they think we can hit them as well?'

'Just rest easy awhile,' Wayne said in a low voice. 'We've got too much to live for to get into a shooting match with a bunch of range rats.'

The term was hardly complimentary, but Cody could

see why it came to mind to describe this ragtag outfit. One of them was a bulky, tall man dressed in furs. His hat was torn, his beard unkempt. He carried a double-barreled shotgun, and seemed to be the patriarch of the group. Of the three others one was tall and slender, dressed in furs and rags. He carried an old Spencer repeating rifle. Between them were two more clan members. They were both wearing ground-dusting skirts so they must have been women, but it was hard to tell at a distance.

It wasn't much easier as they drew nearer, plodding purposefully across the grassland. The larger of the two women wore a blue bandanna over her hair, which trickled in a few iron-gray strands across her broad fore-head. The younger was a mere squirt. She looked about five feet tall, was shod in worn boots and wore a dirty flop hat. She carried a Winchester rifle. Cody would have bet that she was the one who had fired the shot.

They stood before the horsemen, woebegone and dirt-poor but proud. The younger woman's eyes flashed with hatred or remembered grievances. The eyes were a hazy sort of blue-gray; her mouth was small and pouting, her jaw set.

'Y'all get off our land!' the girl said with an anger which throttled her throat and caused her to tremble.

The older man shushed her. 'Sorry about the shoot-ing,' he said, not looking a bit sorry. He stroked his silver-streaked beard as he studied the horsemen and the weapons they were carrying, measuring them. 'You are on private property, you know.'

'We didn't see anything posted,' Wayne, who was

angry, answered. He would take charge as usual. 'There's no fence, no corner marker, nothing. In this country a man takes his right of passage for granted.'

'I still think they're rustlers,' the girl said, rocking excitedly on her feet. The wind shifted the shapeless brown skirt she wore. Her eyes continued to flash warning signals. Her hands still gripped the Winchester tightly. 'I saw them looking our cattle over.'

Charlie spoke up now. 'Ever see a cowhand ride past a stray steer without even looking at it?'

'They ain't stray, they're our'n,' the wide-built older woman said. Her voice creaked as if it had risen from some seldom-used depth of her body. Probably, Cody thought, she was just nervous. She looked to the older man for leadership.

'That was just a manner of speaking,' Wayne said with more unction than was usual with him. Obviously he wanted no trouble with these people. 'The cattle are widely scattered, not bunched. That's all my friend meant. Hard to tell where they came from. A cattleman will always study the brand the beef carries.'

'Ain't branded yet,' the tiny girl said, stepping even nearer. She lifted her face to Wayne. 'No need to slap iron on them – we ain't never had no rustlers out here before.'

These were rough-talking, rough-living, independent folks. Cody had seen nothing like them since the time he had met up with some of the Clinch Mountain boys – a clan of untamed mountain men who had moved from their Appalachian stronghold in the east a few years back to migrate to the west and skipped all civilization along the way. He wondered if these people could be some offshoot of that family of lawless men. He took his turn at trying to calm matters down.

'We're only three wandering men who lost our jobs on the high mountain ranges, due to winter lay-offs. We're trying to make our way to the Triangle in hopes of finding a situation there. We were studying the brands to see if we might be closer to the ranch.'

'Triangle thinks it owns all of the land west of the Pecos and south of the Canadian line,' the younger man, who had not spoken before, said in a peculiar piping voice. The other members of the family nodded their heads in agreement.

'I guess maybe we made a mistake,' the patriarch said after a moment's thought. 'We're kind-of pinched out here, you see. We can't afford to lose an inch of graze or a head of cattle. I guess maybe you're what you say – honest, hard-working men looking for a rack.'

The old man had relaxed a little, as had the younger, thin one. The little girl seemed to be still tightly wound. Cody thought she resembled a child's toy, which if the right lever were pushed would go bounding and tumbling away from them in odd directions, squawking all the way.

'If that's settled,' the plump older woman said, relaxing and revealing her motherly side, 'maybe it would be neighborly to offer these boys a bowl of hot soup and some bread, Emil.'

'Maybe so,' the man, Emil, said uncertainly. 'If they wouldn't have any objection to eating poor fare in poor

41

circumstances.'

'I've eaten in holes in the ground before,' Charlie said unwisely.

'We're not diggers, mister!' the girl spat back. 'We've got a fine house – it just ain't finished yet, as timber and all are hard to come by out here.'

'Hush, Lonnie,' Emil said. 'The man didn't mean nothing. He was just saying he's eaten in all sorts of places when he was hungry enough. No need to brag about our poor house.'

'They're like the Triangle people, looking down their noses at us!' the girl, Lonnie, said moodily.

'Then Triangle isn't far off?' Wayne asked.

'Half a day's ride,' Emil answered, 'but I don't think you boys have enough light to make it today – besides,' he said, lifting his chin toward the north, 'there seems to be a storm right on your heels.'

It was true; the storm clouds they had seen earlier were now stacked high above the mountains, and Cody could see a spike of lightning crease their black, rumpled depths. Thunder made the earth tremble and hurried their decision.

'Looks like we'd better, boys,' he said, and to Emil, 'if you're sure you have the room.'

'We've enough. I'll not leave any man out in this,' Emil said through his beard. The wind had begun to fairly race across the plains and the clouds cast long, menacing shadows. They started on unhurriedly. Though the weather suggested urgency, Emil and his family were afoot and could travel no faster.

'How's your horse?' Emil asked Wayne as they

walked on through the blustering day. 'It seemed that
Lonnie tagged it. There must by a frying pan in your
saddle-bags from the sound it made.'

'I carry implements,' Wayne said tightly. 'The horse
will be all right. It just got spooked.'

'Sometimes Lonnie don't think before she acts,'
Emil said. 'It seems to be a common failing in our
family.'

Wayne just nodded, and both men fell silent as the
thunder roared and the cold wind slapped against
their bodies. The sun was beginning to die in the west
and it painted the underside of the towering storm
clouds a blood red.

Topping a rise now they caught sight of a clump of
live-oak trees, and built among them stood a very long,
very low structure. It was of poles and used lumber,
carelessly fitted together. The roof was sod. One end of
the long house had been daubed with whitewash, but
the material apparently had given out before the other
end was reached. Smoke rose in a flattened curlicue
from a native stone chimney.

Cody felt the tug on his stirrup and looking down he
saw Lonnie walking close beside him. The first cold
drops of rain were beginning to fall and there was a
definite chill to the wind. He looked at her in puzzle-
ment. She trudged on methodically, her eyes kept
straight ahead. What did she want? He was about to ask
her when she whispered above a gust of tree-rattling
wind:

'I was only talking mean to you to drive you away.
When I shot I was just trying to give you warning. I

43

wasn't trying to hit the horse. My shooting's not so good, I guess.'

What was she gabbling on about? No one else was looking their way and Lonnie was still not looking at Cody. The oak trees shuddered in the wind as they passed through them toward the house.

'You should have gone away,' Lonnie whispered. 'Once you're inside the house, they're sure to kill you.'

# FOUR

'Those cattle should have been bunched,' Charlie said over the meal that Mrs Stanton – for that was her name – had provided. The wind and rain had settled in and raced on unabated outside the squat, smoky house. 'Best to keep them together in a storm. Fewer will wander, and it helps them to keep warm.'

'We're not cowhands,' Emil Stanton said loudly but without roughness. 'And we only own one horse – it's used for plowing and hauling.'

Charlie and Wayne nodded in understanding sympathy. Both had been doing the meal justice. It was corn soup and fresh, yeasty bread, which Mrs Stanton had delivered to the table with some pride. The room was long and narrow, the ceiling so low that a tall man like Wayne and the Stanton boy, Luke, had to duck his head to move around in it.

Cody sat at the foot of the long plank table, which could seat eight, and ate with caution, listening to the random conversation. He had not tasted his soup until he saw that everyone else was eating. He caught

Lonnie's eye once across the table and she seemed to nod. She did not smile – Cody wondered if she even knew how – but her look seemed to indicate that there was no poison in the food, although Cody was uncomfortable anyway after her earlier warning.

He hadn't had the chance to tell Wayne and Charlie what Lonnie had said to him. Emil, suddenly the gregarious host, had swept them inside the long house and pointed out things he had done there, what he intended to do once he could come by some cash money from selling some of his cattle.

These, as Wayne, Charlie and Cody had all noticed, were unbranded. The odds were that they were mavericks and probably had once belonged to Triangle, though that would be impossible to prove. There was some grumbling about Triangle around the table from the Stanton family, but this seemed to be based on sheer envy for the most part. People who don't have what someone else has always seem to have a grudge against them. Even though they would like to be exactly like them. Cursing another man's luck, Cody guessed you might call it, though it was seldom luck that made a man profit, but some brains and a lot of hard work.

'Things'll get better around here when Amos and Daltry arrive,' the old woman said, leaning away from the table with satisfaction, her hands resting on her aproned lap. Charlie and Wayne glanced at Emil Stanton for illumination.

'Those are my two older sons,' Emil said, wiping some of his meal from his shaggy gray beard. 'Good

46

strong men. . . .' He glanced at his youngest son, Luke, but did not continue with whatever it was he was thinking.

'Where are they?' Charlie asked. Beyond the house a gust of wind-driven cold rain pelted the house. Automatically they all looked to the flimsy walls.

'We used to have a young redbud tree right off the front porch,' the old woman said, her eyes clouded with remembrance. 'Had a storm like this last winter and it got blown over.'

'The boys,' Emil Dalton told them, 'have been up in the mountains, prospecting for gold. They'll have to give it up with this weather settling in. It would be fine if they made a strike, wouldn't it, Mother?' Emil said to his wife. 'Even a small one Then we could make some improvements around here.'

'Maybe get some cloth to make a dress,' Lonnie said, though no one but Cody seemed to hear her or pay attention to her. The girl was a mystery, like one of those wooden Chinese puzzles that seemed so simple until you tried to put it together.

She had seemed wildcat tough at first. Then she had warned Cody of trouble brewing, seeming deeply concerned for the visitors. She had ranted and shouted out on the range. Inside the house she had hardly made a peep. Cody deliberately let his eyes meet hers from time to time, but there was no way to read her inner thoughts. She ate in silence, her eyes fixed on her bowl.

After Lonnie and her mother had cleared away the dinner dishes, Emil Dalton lit a long-stemmed pipe he had filled with black tobacco. They sat on leather-bottomed chairs near a low-burning fire, Emil rocking back and forth, a distant smile on his lips. 'Things will be better when Amos and Daltry get back from the mountains. Their little bit of gold will be enough to help us through the hard winter.' He looked briefly thoughtful, concerned, as he puffed on his pipe.

'Cash money is always a help, isn't it?' he asked, looking directly at Wayne, who had not helped suspicions by insisting on having his saddle-bags under his chair during supper and who now had them resting beside his left hand.

'I suppose,' Wayne answered easily, 'though I've never had enough to know.'

'No, a cowhand seldom gets rich, does he?' Emil asked.

'No.'

'Well, let's hope your sons have had some luck,' Charlie said, speaking up, perhaps not liking the turn the conversation was taking. 'Are you expecting them soon?'

'I am,' Emil said, 'but you never know in weather like this, do you? It's a long walk back from . . . the place they were trying to work.'

'They're walking?' Cody asked. Emil's eyes shifted toward him. In a far corner, Cody saw the shadowy figure of Lonnie moving around.

'They're walking. I told you, we don't have but one horse. We're not rich, remember? Oh, they've got that jackass for toting their ore and supplies, nothing else.'

Something about this response bothered Cody –

48

perhaps the idea that a man as poor as Emil Stanton
was would feel wealthy if he owned three good horses.
Did he covet their animals?

Enough to kill for them?

'It's tough up in those mountains,' Wayne said for
something to say. His craggy face was intent in the firelight as if he too had been warned by Emil's remarks.
The saddle-bags containing their gold remained within
reach of his left hand. His holster remained within
reach of his right.

Luke Stanton, who had lounged against the wall
near the fireplace, silent until now, said:

'Those mountains are rough, all right. I went up
there once with my Uncle Morris, trapping for furs. I
almost died three or four times. I guess he did die.'

All three of the visitors came alert. Charlie asked
without indicating his interest, 'Who was Uncle Morris?
What happened?'

'He was my brother,' Emil Stanton said, knocking
the dottle from his pipe into his palm. 'He was sure he
was going to get rich on furs.'

'He was a trapper?' Charlie asked. Emil looked at
him as if that was the most stupid question he had ever
heard.

'That's what I said,' Emil said stonily. 'Went off one
winter; probably got himself froze to death. Never saw
him again. But that's been years ago.' The old man got
to his feet.

'If you boys will excuse me, I'm tired. Lonnie will show
you where to bunk down. Mother!' he called. 'It's
bedtime.' In a quieter, flatter voice, he said to the visitors,

'Men, nothing against your company, but I intend to find you've gone in the morning, storm or none.'

Then he turned and shuffled off toward the rear of the house, his plump wife rushing after him, still drying her hands on a dish towel. Lonnie followed her mother into the room, her eyes somber, her motions measured as if she were trying to remain calm, in control of her emotions.

'I'll show you where you can sleep,' the girl said. Charlie rose; Wayne shouldered his heavy saddle-bags which gave out an unhoped-for clink. The three men followed her down a dark hall. Opening a door she reached into her skirt pocket, produced a candle stub and lighted it. She led them into the room.

'This will have to do for two of you,' Lonnie said, handing the candle to Charlie. There were low, leather-strapped beds on either side of the small room. 'This is my brothers' room. Amos and Daltry. They shouldn't be back tonight – of course if they do make it through the storm we'll have to figure something else out.'

The storm still banged and thundered around the house. If Amos and Daltry were walking through it, they'd deserve their own dry beds, Cody thought. Lonnie hesitated before turning toward Cody. 'This way,' she told him as Charlie placed the fat candle carefully on a plate set on a low puncheon table which was already marked with candle drippings. Lonnie led the way down the dark hall again and opened a narrow door.

'This is only a storeroom,' she said. 'But it's drier than it is outside.' She withdrew another candle from her skirt pocket and lit it.

'It's fine,' Cody said in the near darkness. He thought he could hear her breathing, shallow and a little excited. He would make a bed of a pile of burlap sacking stacked in the storeroom. It was better than the open plains by far.

'Was there something else?' Lonnie asked Cody.

'I don't know. Is there?'

She hesitated. 'I don't suppose so. I'll leave the door open so that you can see what you're doing.'

Cody nodded and watched as the slender, forlorn girl walked away. He waited until he could no longer hear the sound of her boot-heels clicking down the hall, then slipped out of the storeroom to return to where Charlie and Wayne were making their beds.

With a soft tap he entered to find both men fully dressed and alert. Charlie, perched on the bed, looked especially uneasy. They looked up at him.

'Well, Cody, what do you think?' Wayne asked.

'I think we've gotten ourselves into serious trouble,' Cody answered, and he went on to tell them about Lonnie's warning.

'They mean to kill us?' Charlie said, startled by the idea. He glared at Wayne. 'I knew you were giving those saddle-bags too much attention!'

'No one was paying any mind,' Wayne protested.

'It was the sound of the bullet striking metal that alerted them,' Cody believed. 'The girl, Lonnie, apologized, saying she was a poor shot, that it was an accident. I doubt it – I think it was deliberate.'

'Who knows?' Charlie said dismally. 'Who knows if

she was telling the truth? She doesn't seem to be the most stable person I've ever come across. Maybe she was just having fun with you, Cody.'

'Some fun,' Cody muttered, glancing into the dark hallway behind him.

Wayne rubbed his hand across his head. He wondered, 'What about these two sons – Amos and Daltry? Do they even exist? Are they lurking around here somewhere, and not gone away as the old man told us?'

'Prospecting!' Charlie said in disparagement. His round face was morose in the candlelight. 'I never heard of no gold up above the Rios Canyon. If there was, there'd be a hundred men up there searching for it.'

'Maybe that wasn't the kind of gold they were prospecting for,' Wayne said. He was silent for a minute, then he suggested quite deliberately, 'Maybe they have been looking for gold that has already been refined and minted.'

'The gold that belonged to the trapper?' Cody asked. 'Do you think he might have been this mysterious Uncle Morris they mentioned?'

'Who knows?' Wayne answered, shifting his eyes as a small sound outside caught his ear.

'Even if this Morris was the trapper, how could anyone have known that he had come into money in a card game?' Charlie asked. Wayne shrugged.

'He could have sent a note with a passer-by,' Cody suggested.

'That doesn't seem likely. I doubt if any of this bunch can read or write anyway. We probably are letting our imaginations run away with us,' Wayne countered. 'Maybe they would be willing to kill us for out horses and whatever's in our pockets – dirt poor as this Stanton family seems to be.'

'There might not be any brothers,' Charlie said as if clinging to that idea. 'Just something they made up to worry us.'

'It don't matter. Once we fall asleep that old man can take care of us all with his shotgun,' Wayne said.

'There's three of them who are armed,' Charlie said miserably. He paused for a minute, listening to the hard-driving rain against the roof. 'I'd rather not wake up dead tomorrow. What do you think we should do, Wayne?'

'We could take turns standing watch all night,' Wayne said with a tight shake of his head, 'but for myself I'm thinking…' He looked up. 'We ought to get away from this place as fast as possible.'

There was no debate. Not a man wished to go out into a fierce winter storm where all sorts of calamities were possible, but the alternative to rough travel was spending the night in a house where they had already been warned that they would be killed before dawn. They had endured rough traveling before – none of them had yet survived his own murder.

They decided to make their break for it now rather than wait until the dead of night. The storm would get no better, and the mysterious brothers, Daltry and Amos, might arrive to aid in the killing of the travelers. Wayne lugged his heavy saddle-bags across his shoulder and all three men carried weapons in their hands as they slunk down the dark corridor toward the front door.

They nearly walked into Lonnie Stanton.

The slender girl's eyes opened wide, but she did not make a sound, as they feared; she simply backed away deeper into the murky shadows of the smoky house. Wayne jerked his head toward the front door and they went that way in a bunch. The wind was howling, the rain driving down. Once the door to the house was flung open the sound increased to a tumult. They had to fight their way against the wind through the iron mesh of the rain. They were frozen to the bone within minutes as they slogged toward the horses through the inches-deep mud.

There was no visibility except by the light of the brilliantly flashing lightning. This was sporadic and disorienting, More than once Cody stumbled over an unseen object, and twice went to his knees as they slipped and slid onward. No one had lighted a candle or lantern in the house; no one had raised an alarm.

Once aboard their horses, a few minutes' ride would put them beyond range of visibility in the turmoil of the night. No one would be taking any long shots at them. And with no horses to follow on, the Stantons would be unable to pursue even if they were willing to do so.

All remained quiet inside the house; no shout of warning followed them. The storm raged and the heavy rain fell from out of the inky sky – and all of this being done because of the whispered warning of an unstable girl. Maybe she had simply been 'having fun' with Cody.

'Let's go,' Wayne urged them from horseback, 'before the brothers show up.'

'What brothers?' Charlie snarled. 'We ain't never seen them,' he said, still holding to his theory that Daltry and Amos might be imaginary. 'Besides, if they're walking home through this weather, they won't so much as see us, let alone have an idea of what's going on.'

Cody swung into his saddle leather. Oddly, he agreed with both men. Like Charlie, he did not believe that any men arriving on foot out of the darkness of the wintry night would be willing or able to start a fight with strangers without provocation.

Like Wayne, he thought that the best thing to do was to escape from the Stanton place as rapidly as possible. Thunder rolled across the long plains, lightning struck perilously close as they made their way from the yard of the house. Rain drove violently down. By the time they were out of sight of the house the darkness was so complete that Cody could not make out his fellow travelers in the whirl and thrust of the storm. They were completely obscured in a blackness of the prairie night.

That was why it was such a surprise when the first rifle bullet was fired from out of the darkness, striking flesh.

# FIVE

Charlie Tuttle let out a yowl and his horse bucked furiously. Cody could no longer see him although they had been riding through the dark storm nearly side by side. There was nothing but the night, the pelting rain and the gunman's threat.

'Charlie!' Cody circled back, his eyes searching the ground at his horse's feet, but although he thought he could hear a man's moans above the roar and rush of the storm, he could not find Charlie. Another bullet from out of the darkness halted his search. Cody felt his buckskin buckle at the knees and then pitch forward. Kicking out of his stirrups, Cody leaped to the ground to move away from the weight of the dying horse. Another bullet was fired, but this one seemed to miss him by a wide margin, but then perhaps Cody had not been the target.

Who was the shooting man? How could his rifle be so accurate when they could barely see through the gloom of the stormy night?

Cody took a wrong step and slipped to his knees.

Rising from the sodden ground he slipped and stumbled his way forward, seeking some sort of shelter. As he went he called out again:

'Charlie! Wayne?'

There was no answer. His knee knocked into something solid and he went down over it. It was a fallen cottonwood tree he hadn't seen in the darkness. He hunkered down behind it, pistol in hand. The rain beat down the brim of his hat and he was forced to bow his head as the constant cold wind stung his eyes.

What was there to do? Without his horse, with a gunman behind him and his friends lost or dead, there was very little choice. He could strike out toward the Triangle ranch on foot, but he had no idea how far it was or if he could find it in this darkness. Nor, disoriented as he was just then, could he even be sure of the direction he needed to travel. But his mind's image was of faceless riflemen finding him in the darkness of the storm and finishing him off.

He did not call out again; he didn't want to lead any of the killers to him.

One thought cheered him slightly: if it was the Stanton brothers who were shooting – and it nearly had to be – they were also supposedly afoot, and they had traveled long that day already. With that faintly cheering thought in mind, he started on, away from the wind toward what should be southward, since the storm was blowing in from the north. The cold ground underfoot was goo. He slogged and slipped onward. Once he nearly walked into an oak tree in the darkness; twice he went down as he stepped into unseen dips, twisting his ankle and tearing hide from his knee on a rock.

He was cold, stunned and alone. The rain and wind continued unabated, the storm showing no mercy. Cody staggered on like a blind man. The only warmth he could feel was from blood trickling down his leg from his torn knee. His situation could not get much grimmer.

And then it did.

He tripped over the dead man in the darkness and fell again. He landed face first against the cold mud. In panic he sat up and turned toward the dead man. Lightning flashed and by its garish light Cody recognized the face of Wayne Tucker. There was a streak of black blood across his forehead and down over one open eye. The other dead eye stared blankly up into the rain. Wayne's saddle-bags lay near his outstretched fingers, the leather sodden. Ashamed for sparing so little time for pity, Cody wondered where Wayne's horse had gotten to. He told himself that Wayne was of no use to him then, whereas his horse was. It was a savage sort of survival instinct which drove the shameful but necessary thought.

Cody rose, taking the saddle-bags with him. He peered around in vain in the darkness, searching for Wayne's horse, but could not find it. Probably it had been shot or had wandered off. It might have been captured by the sniper.. This last worried him the most. The sky would clear some time; the sun would shine again and he would be afoot on the wide plains while the killer, now mounted, would be able to ride him down easily.

Staggering on as thunder rumbled again, close enough to rattle his eardrums, he started toward the south once more. There was a coulee to the east, he knew, for they had crossed it en route to the Stanton house, but then they had been following someone who knew the trail well. Crossing that sandy cut would not be easy in the darkness, and probably the coulee was filled with rushing water by now.

He slogged on, his legs heavy, his knee throbbing and starting to stiffen, his ankle wrenched. The night was turbulent, the skies dark and confused. As for Cody his confusion was as deep. He was not even sure what had happened, who had been shooting at them, how they had found the three travelers. He shambled on, his clothing heavy with rain, the gold-weighted saddle-bags cutting a crease in the flesh of his shoulder.

The shadowy figure was suddenly there before him. Bright eyes studied Cody's approach warily. For an instant Cody believed he had found Wayne's gray horse, but it was not. A dun-colored burro stood miserably in the rain. On its back was a ragged pack; a lead rope was attached to its white muzzle. The animal did not shy away as Cody approached it. It seemed too weary and storm-beaten to run. No wonder: if it was the jackass that had belonged to the Stanton brothers, it had already been led all the way from Rios Canyon through the teeth of the storm.

'Sorry to do this,' Cody muttered, 'but I've a use for you.'

It was the job of only a few minutes to remove the pack from the little animal's back and let the Stanton brothers' gear fall to the muddy ground. The canvas pack rattled as if it contained pots and pans, maybe a coffee pot, but there could have been little else in it. It was light, far too light to be containing any ore.

The burro shuddered with relief. Perhaps it was thinking that this human would now get him out of the storm, rub him down and bring food. It got none of this treatment; there was none to give. Instead Cody draped the heavy saddle-bags over its back, took its lead rope and walked the donkey onward.

He had thought briefly of trying to ride the dumb animal, and it probably would have carried him, but how far? He instead simply trudged forward, pulling the reluctant little beast after him, carrying its burden into the drape of frozen darkness. As the rain settled in once more and each step became a small battle, with no sign of lessening, no indication of shelter ahead, Cody's inconsequential thought was:

*The skeleton has won the last hand again.*

He came upon the winding coulee at last. As he had expected, water rushed rapidly through the sandy cut that time and centuries of earlier storms had gouged across the face of the prairie. Hesitating, Cody Hawk started the burro down into the cut following a path formed by a landslide. Below, the river raged; above, the sky rumbled. They would not cross the coulee bottom, not on this night, but what Cody was hoping for was some respite from the wind, some shelter from the driving storm.

He slipped on the uncertain footing and again fell. The sure-footed burro stood, ears twitching, studying

Cody as he struggled to his feet in the ankle-deep sand. Again lightning forked across the sky, briefly revealing the coulee bottom. White water frothed southward. There was a narrow bank above the water and not far along it a dark hollow which might be deep enough to shelter in, however slight its protection might be. Anything in the way of cover would be welcome.

Struggling upward again to reach the bench Cody found the hollow in the sandy bank. It was no more than five feet deep, and from its roof dangled the roots of a tree which would soon be toppled by the storm. Would the bank cave in and leave Cody smothered? No matter, for now it was a place where the cold wind did not cut through his clothes and the rain was not driven like buckshot into his face. Cody crawled into the enclosure, which smelled of damp sand and tree root.

He sat panting for a time, legs drawn up. Beyond the opening to the tiny cave, lightning struck again, illuminating the tumbling sky and constant rush of rain. Cody could see nothing around him in the darkness, but then there wasn't much to see. He tried once and once only to urge the donkey to follow him into the tight confines of the recess, but unlike a man, the burro could not duck down and curl up. With one disdainful look, the animal drew away on its lead rope, preferring to stand in the rain. No matter – trying to shelter up together would have made for an uncomfortable night for both of them, and at least the burro was out of the wind where it stood.

Cody tied the tethering rope around his ankle and lay back, exhausted and cold, trying not to think of what had passed and of tomorrow, but only of long-distant pleasant times. At last, despite the tumult of the night and the bone-chilling cold, he did at some point fall asleep, nudged out of the real world by his utter weariness.

Cody awoke to an unreal world. He sat up suddenly and tendrils of roots brushed across his face. There was a cold, brilliant shimmering in the opening to the cave and something was tugging at his foot. He rubbed a hand across his head to brush the roots away and found that his hair was matted with damp sand. He searched around for his hat, peering into the brilliance of the rising sun. The burro was moving around, probably trying to find some graze. Cody knew the animal could not have been fed for a long while, possibly for days. Sitting cross-legged on the sandy floor of the cave, he untied the tether from his ankle and then crawled to the cave entrance.

Below he could see the river still raging southward. Above, the sky was clouded, but these were broken clouds, the sun glinting on their skirts, making them into silver angels, not a dark assaulting force.

Cody tried to rise to his feet, but his injured knee buckled, and he nearly fell to the ground, saving himself only by grabbing hold of the steady little burro. The saddle-bags were still in place. The rain could have done no harm to their contents. After a long look around and a sigh, Cody started on again, leading the burro down the sandy path.

The rushing river water was loud in his ears. There

without complaint or balkiness. The same could not be said for horses, Cody thought with a faded smile, recalling the many time his buckskin pony had nearly refused to acknowledge its master's behests out of what seemed to be sheer obstinacy.

The land continued long and empty, the skies cold and gray. But now they often came across ponds left by the rain, and the grass, though not flourishing, grew there. The burro at least could be fed and watered at intervals. Cody preceded the animal to water and drank his fill of the muddy water, lying on his belly, rinsing his filthy face. Then as the jackass filled its stomach with the bunch grass near by, Cody would take long minutes to survey his backtrail and to look ahead hopefully.

Once, while resting, Cody thought he saw sun glinting off metal in the far western distances, and peering that way with anxious eyes, he thought that he could see a lone horseman across the plains. It was impossible to be certain at that distance, which was over a mile, but he thought that it was the lone rider he had first spotted following them back along Rios Canyon. Perhaps that was just a notion. In any event, it made no difference; the horseman was not closing and in another minute he had vanished once more.

So long as he was not one of the Stanton brothers Cody supposed it didn't matter who the rider was. He could have even been an outrider from Triangle, for now Cody knew that he was coming closer to the vast ranch. He began passing stray cattle, probably scattered by the rainstorm, healthy-looking steers and at least one cow with a nursing red calf. All except the calf wore the simple, distinctive Triangle brand. They showed no interest in the passing of a stranger. Placidly they continued to shear grass as Cody limped past followed by the equally stoic donkey.

The sun was overhead by now and a strange mist was rising from the plains – a ground fog caused by the heating of the damp earth returning moisture to the sky. It was still cool when the wind blew, but oddly warm and humid as the sun rode high and the fog grew dense.

Cody marched doggedly on, hoping for some sign of working men or ranch buildings. For all he knew he had strayed badly off course, but there was no choice but to continue as he had been. Even the poorest of settlements, a lone sod house where he could purchase a meal and pause long enough to look at his damaged knee, would have been welcome. There had to be some sort of town near by, but he didn't know in which direction it lay. He knew that there would be a town, because a huge ranch like Triangle needed supplies and services on a constant basis, and in many places towns were thrown up near by only to serve the ranches and their working men. That had been the genesis of the small town of McCormack, which served the Domino ranch, fed liquor to its cowhands and offered crude diversions to them as the town provided services to the ranch proper. There were flour mills, hay and grain stores, hardware shops, bootmakers in McCormack, even a poor two-room infirmary. Services even the most self-sustaining ranches could not provide.

Thinking along these lines, Cody had halted the burro once and almost guiltily opened the saddle-bags it carried. He slipped a few gold pieces from them and shamefully tucked them into his pockets. If he happened upon an opportunity for food and rest, he meant to be able to pay his way. He was stealing from no one; still, he felt as if he were pilfering from Wayne and Charlie or perhaps robbing the skeleton hand of its just possessions.

He staggered on, wondering if he were not growing a little delirious. The gold gave him small comfort. He wanted to find a shack, a grove of trees, a bite of food, a place out of the weather. He removed his hat and wiped his eyes free of perspiration with his kerchief.

Still, as he kept his eyes fixed on the horizon ahead, he would take an occasional worried look back the way he had come, but he saw no one following him. That suited Cody – he was in no shape to put up much of a fight if he were attacked. His stiff leg had reduced his pace to a hobble. He was light-headed from hunger, his vision blurry from long hours of squinting into the sun.

The sun sank lower at his back. Looking that way Cody could see it glinting off the snow that had recently fallen in the high mountains, coloring it brightly. He had no more than two hours before sunset, possibly less. The wind still blew hard and he knew he was facing another desperately cold night in the open once the ball of the sun rolled off the table in the west.

He trudged on with his head down, each step causing a bludgeoning pain in his knee. He had developed a heavy, throbbing headache. His shadow was long before him when he again glanced up and saw them coming.

Four horsemen in a ragged line were approaching him from out of the east. They had to be Triangle riders, didn't they? Perhaps looking for the scattered steers he had seen earlier. They rode with deliberation like cavalry soldiers approaching a battle. Their hats were tugged low against the glare of the dying sun. Cody halted and let them approach. If these were Triangle cowhands, the worst of his nightmare was ended.

If they were enemies, this hour on the plains could prove to be his last.

# SIX

Someone among the riders raised a gloved hand and pointed toward Cody Hawk, and all four men started toward him, spreading out a little. At a distance Cody could not make out the brands of the horses they rode, but he felt certain that these were Triangle riders. He stood in place, leaning a shoulder against the side of the burro. Weariness and pain had taken their toll on him. He needed the animal's support.

These were hard-bitten men, their faces sun-weathered and serious. The man who seemed to be their leader, the man riding at the head of the group, was not recently shaven. A wild, graying blond mustache flourished untrimmed on his stern face. The brim of his hat was folded far down in front, hiding his eyes from the setting sun. Reining in his sorrel horse roughly, he glared down at Cody and demanded:

'What's your name?'

'Cody Hawk.'

'He just made that up,' the slender man at his side said. Despite the weather he was wearing a badly shaped straw hat with a blue bandanna as a hatband.

'Maybe,' their leader agreed, 'but he don't resemble any of those thieving Stantons.' He then asked:

'Do you know the Stantons, Mr Cody Hawk?'

'I ran across them,' Cody admitted. 'Back there.' He nodded his head vaguely east. 'I can't say I took to them. Listen,' Cody continued while the men exchanged glances and murmurs. 'I'm nothing but a rambling cowboy. . . .'

'You can tell by that fine cutting horse he's got,' one of the outriders jibed.

Cody continued with a weak smile. 'Three of us got fired off the Domino ranch last week. Domino doesn't keep much of a winter crew. We thought we'd make our way down out of the mountains to try finding a new situation.'

'Who's foreman up on Domino?' the narrow man in straw asked challengingly.

'Boss Allison,' Cody answered. Their leader still stared icily at him, but Cody could tell they were starting to believe him.

'He could have heard the name anywhere,' the inquisitor said. The man had taken an instant dislike to Cody for reasons he could not fathom.

'Be quiet, Ned,' their mustached leader ordered. 'Let me ask some questions.'

'Sure, Walt,' the man in the straw hat, Ned, answered sullenly.

'Cody, did you see any Triangle cattle over that way? On the Stanton place, I mean.'

'I didn't see any branded cattle,' Cody said honestly.

'They're picking us clean,' the man named Ned erupted. He was red-faced now, trembling. 'Bunch of scavengers! Picking us clean.'

Cody said, 'There's a scattered bunch of Triangle cows not two miles ahead. I did pass them.'

'We'd better gather them and push them east before the Stantons get all of them too,' Ned said excitedly.

'Get after them,' their mustached boss, Walt, said as if with resignation. 'You haven't got much time to do it on this day,' he remarked, looking skyward, toward the setting sun. He gave a signal to the other two men, and in a bunch they started westward. Walt remained behind briefly.

'Pay no attention to Ned Pierce,' Walt said. 'He takes the loss of a single head of Triangle cattle seriously. Not that I don't . . .' He paused, leaned forward in the saddle and extended a gloved hand. 'The name's Walt Donovan. I'm Triangle foreman. We may be able to use you, Cody. I'll talk to the boss. If you keep going the way you are, you'll likely reach Triangle before dark. If not, walk into the rising moon and you'll be on course. You've lost your horse and outfit, have you?'

'In the storm,' Cody answered, not wanting to go into the whole story.

'Yeah – that's tough weather in the high mountains, I know. I once worked up in that country myself, on Matchbox. I knew Boss Allison when we were both just kids. Has he lost all of his hair yet?'

'Not unless he shaved it off,' Cody answered, recognizing the trick to trap him for what it was. Allison had the beard and hair of an unshorn bull buffalo.

71

Donovan laughed and flagged his thumb back across his shoulder. 'Straight ahead, as I told you. I doubt you'll make it for supper, though.'

So did Cody. He watched as Donovan wheeled his fine sorrel horse and rode off after the others. It was a long trek he still faced, but Cody could not help but feel better than he had been. He was near to the Triangle ranch and had been given at least a tentative promise of work by the ranch foreman.

'Let's go,' Cody said to the donkey. 'With luck we'll both find feed and shelter on this night.'

Cody now led the burro across broad grasslands dotted with scattered oak trees. He came upon more shorthorn cattle, and at sundown saw a man in a hay wagon plying his pitchfork to drop extra fodder to the cattle bunched around him. This man halted in his motion, raised a hand to Cody, removed his hat and wiped his brow with his cuff. His wagon was nearly empty, the sun red in the west, and he was obviously ready to return home.

'Got a ride for me?' Cody asked as he wearily approached the wagon, nudging the steers aside. The man looked down and nodded.

'You look like you could use one,' he said with a smile. 'Going to Triangle, are you? Hop on back then; I'll get you there.'

Most men in the far country were friendly. They saw few strangers, but they treated each as a friend until he proved himself to be otherwise. Now, seated on the rough planking of the wagon bed, leading the burro as the wagon turned and headed back toward the home ranch, Cody felt more at ease than he had for days. The dying sun colored the bottoms of the still-prevalent clouds, but the cruel wind had subsided with sunset. It was growing chill again, but Cody Hawk had every hope of finding himself in a warm bunkhouse before nightfall.

He watched as the wagon drove on, parting the multitude of cattle. There were hundreds of them in this quarter alone, maybe thousands. Triangle was prospering beyond most men's dreams, certainly far beyond those of a poor squatter like Emil Stanton, explaining his envy.

What Stanton and others like him did not seem to understand was that someone had come here and made his success through hard work and attention to detail, expanding slowly, deliberately planning his every move. To Emil their success was because the Triangle owners were there first and had taken all of the prime land, leaving nothing left for settlers like him.

There was some truth to that, but if Stanton were to work his own small herd patiently and knowledgeably, in time he would achieve at least some small level of prosperity. Cody in passing had seen no sign that the Stantons knew cattle or had the ambition required to tend them. He did not doubt that the Stanton herd was mostly maverick Triangle stock, but that could not be proved on open range. And Stanton had so far neglected even the rudimentary task of slapping his own brand on the cattle so that his ownership could not be challenged.

What did it matter to Cody? No one was paying him for his advice. The wagon rolled on, jolting beneath him. The burro tagged along almost cheerfully as if it sensed that feed and shelter lay somewhere ahead.

What did Cody care about the Stantons! Nothing. They had run him off and tried to kill him.

Why then was he finding himself thinking of Lonnie as he rode the wagon? She was a little wildcat with a sharp mouth. True, she had warned them and helped them escape, but probably she did not want them murdered in the house where she would have to clean up the mess. No, Cody's thoughts of the girl were only those of a lonesome man too long alone in the wild country. Like some cowboy singing a song about the girl he left behind in Abilene – the girl who had not given the dumb cowboy so much as a thought once he was out of sight.

Men on horseback passed them as they approached the main ranch. Cody had to turn his head to look ahead and see the two-story white house, its face bright with sunset flush in the gloomy hour of dusk.

Horses nickered and rubbed shoulders in a corral as they passed. Smoke curled upward from an unseen source, carrying the scents of frying beef. Cody felt a small flush of fear: there was something he had neglected to do, and now he meant to take care of it before it could become a fatal error. He had all of that gold with him; it had to be hidden safely away.

Making a decision, he slid from the back of the wagon, raising a hand to the surprised driver, and walked the burro into the dark shadows of the oak trees surrounding house and barn. Men would kill for that much money. He had already seen one dead man who had been careless with it and paid the price. Besides, Cody had not like the way that the Triangle man, Ned Pierce, had been studying the saddle-bags when they had met along the trail. There was a malevolent gleam in the eyes of the man with the straw hat, but then perhaps it was habitual.

There was still enough purple light to see by, but the trouble was, Cody did not know exactly where he was. He could make out the layout well enough: main house, barn, smoke rising from an unseen bunkhouse pipe, horse pens. Men walked their horses past him among the trees, joking and grumbling. Apparently on their way to supper. Cody cringed away from them. A lost stranger, especially one leading a burro, would be noticed.

Somewhere a yard dog barked sharply, but it was nowhere near Cody. He moved through the cold shadows of the wind-shifted trees, making his way into the darkness away from the house, which had now come to life with lanterns glowing in many of its windows. With his eyes moving in all directions, Cody finally found what he was looking for. Not far beyond what seemed to be a disused chicken coop there was a stack of granite boulders, apparently left there when the house property was originally cleared for building.

Furtively, Cody slipped the saddle-bags from the puzzled burro's back and carried them to the jumbled stack of rocks. By the last dull illumination of the dead sun, he worked his way around the pile and found a group of head-sized rocks blocking a crevice between the larger stones. He rolled these aside, dancing away as one of them nearly landed on his toes, and wedged the saddle-bags into the crevice, replacing the smaller rocks nearly as they had been.

That would do for the time being. It would have to. Standing back, hands on hips, he studied his work, then gathered up the burro's lead, walking it back toward the barn.

There was a lantern lit inside the barn as Cody Hawk, leading the dun burro, limped into the clean, well-maintained barn. Rows of curious horses looked at him over the gates to their stalls. A chubby man with a cheerful face and a dead stubby pipe between his teeth came forward to meet Cody, a broom in his hand.

'Rowland,' the man said, offering his hand before saying another word. 'Joe Rowland. Some folks call me "Rowly Poley",' he chuckled, pinching the extra accumulated fat around his middle.

'Which do you prefer?' Cody asked.

'Don't matter a bit to me, son. I'm hard to insult. I've learned that taking offense easily can make life rougher than it needs to be. Water off a duck, you know . . . what did you say your name was?'

'Cody Hawk. I just got here,' he said to Rowland, who was petting the muzzle of the donkey.

'I can see that,' Joe Rowland replied. 'What did you say the name of this little animal is?'

'I don't know if it even has one,' Cody said and the cheerful little man wagged his head.

'A shame – everyone deserves a name, and I include

animals, of course.'

'Right now I guess I'd have to call him Hungry,' Cody said. 'The same would do for me.'

'Long trail, was it?' Joe Rowland asked, slipping the tether from 'Hungry's' head.

'Long enough. We came down from Domino, which is up in—'

'I know where Domino is,' Joe said. 'Got the sack, did you? They could at least furnish you boys with some trail grub to see you through.'

'It wasn't their fault. We got caught in the storm and got turned around. Lost our ponies.'

'Looking for a position on Triangle, are you?' Joe Rowland asked.

'Yes. I met Walt Donovan along the trail and he told me to come on in. Said they might have a job for me.'

'If Walt said that, they probably do.' To the burro he said, 'Come along, Hungry. We'll find you a place to bed down.'

They walked along the corridor of the barn. Some of the horses stabled there tried to nuzzle Cody as he passed. One ugly old hammer-headed red roan tried to nip at him. Joe Rowland saw it and laughed.

'That's Beggar. He's got a nasty temper.'

'How do things work here?' Cody asked as Joe led the burro into an empty stall littered with clean straw and turned Hungry around. 'I mean horses – do you have to provide your own, or. . . ?'

'Almost everyone has his own pony, but there's plenty of call for spares – at round-up time, for example, or on a trail drive – so Triangle keeps them around when called for.' Joe paused and smiled as he fed Hungry a handful of green alfalfa hay. 'I guess if the burro was all you had, you'll be needing a horse. And saddle?'

'If such can be provided,' Cody said, shamefaced. 'I lost my horse as I told you – shot from under me.'

'Was it?' Rowland asked with what seemed to be genuine concern. 'Did that happen to involve the Stantons? No,' Joe Rowland laughed at Cody's expression, 'I'm not a mind-reader, but everyone on Triangle knows the Stantons for what they are.'

'I wish we had before we met up with them,' Cody said.

'Well, don't worry, son. We'll fix you up as best we can. A man can't be going around without a horse. Now, I have this three-year-old pinto pony that—'

'Wait a minute, Joe!' Cody halted in front of a stall where the gray horse stood, watching him balefully. 'This is my horse!' For it was Wayne Tucker's pony he saw standing there.

'No it ain't,' a voice from the doorway croaked. 'That's my horse, stranger! Stand away from it!'

There was something bantering in the tone and when Cody turned that way he saw Charlie Tuttle standing there, his arm in a sling, a grin on his round face.

'Charlie!' Cody stared at him.

'Thought you'd managed to lose me, did you?' Charlie offered his left hand in greeting and the two clasped warmly if awkwardly.

'I knew you got shot, but I couldn't find you,' Cody said. 'Then they tagged old Buck and I was thrown. I found Wayne but not his horse.'

'Did Wayne have the. . . ?' Charlie asked, his eyes brightening.

'I'll tell you later,' Cody said, glancing at Joe Rowland, who was busy sweeping and apparently paying no attention to them, but you never knew.

Charlie continued, 'I found Wayne's horse but couldn't find Wayne or you. I mounted up and rode through the night toward Triangle. I figured I'd meet you on the trail if you'd made it.'

'I had to hole up overnight,' Cody said.

'Had I been able to find a place, I would have too,' Charlie answered. 'Tell me, Cody – where's you come by that burro? It's the Stantons', isn't it?'

'It has to be. I just stumbled across it and used it to tote . . .' he glanced again at Joe Rowland, still going cheerfully about his work, 'the gear Wayne was carrying.'

Charlie nodded knowledgeably. 'I guess we'd better talk about that later. Say, let me take you around and introduce you to the boys in the bunkhouse. I'm an old-timer here now. I've been around since breakfast!'

The harsh wind gusted against the open barn door and an extended shadow crossed the floor. They looked up to see Ned Pierce standing there, holding his horse's reins, his straw hat tugged low. His eyes glared at them and he grumbled, 'Just what we need, more dead weight around here.'

'Just looking to work,' Cody replied and wished he hadn't. Ned's dark eyes scowled beneath heavy brows.

'You know what I think of you? I think you're a

Stanton man – where else did you get that burro? I think you're a rustler, and you're up to no good on Triangle.'

His voice had dropped to a heavy pant. Now as Joe approached and took the reins to Pierce's horse from him, he turned and faced Cody directly.

'I want you off this ranch. Now!'

'Walt Donovan told me . . .' Cody protested.

'Donovan ain't here! I'm telling you what to do, and that is to haul your ass off of Triangle.'

'He hasn't even seen the boss yet,' Charlie said, trying to intervene.

'And he won't. Just because they hired you on, cripple, though God knows why. . . .'

'Because I know cattle, Pierce, and so does the kid here,' Charlie said, growing angry. 'I worked alongside him for three years up on the Domino.'

'Why don't you head back up there?' Ned Pierce demanded. Behind him Cody could see Joe Rowland calmly unsaddling Ned's horse, readying it for its stall. Joe seemed to accept Ned's bullying as an everyday occurrence; perhaps it was.

'Listen, Ned,' Cody said in a placating voice.

'I'll not listen to you. I've told you what's expected. I want you to comply. Get aboard your burro and head back to the Stantons.' He stepped nearer, his fists bunched, his mouth set savagely.

Cody knew it was no good trying to reason with the man. Ned was hungry for a fight; nothing else would satisfy him. Cody was trail-weary; his leg was shot through with fiery pain, but he knew that Ned would not settle this amicably, and Cody did not like to be backed into a corner. Weary as he was, his hackles had risen.

'I'm already getting tired of you, Pierce,' Cody said. 'Let's settle this if you haven't got the sense to think it through.'

'That's all I was waiting for,' Ned Pierce said, and the tall man stepped in, fists bunched, face set.

# SEVEN

Cody watched Ned Pierce as he placed his hat aside and plodded forward again. Cody had been in a few fights back on Domino and seen many more. What he had learned from these was that a blustering adversary usually figured to simply wade in and end the fight with his first few blows. When this did not happen, he seemed to take a mental step backwards and flail around in confusion.

Ned Pierce did not seem to be that sort of fighter. He raised his fists and approached quite methodically, not throwing wild punches, but searching for an opening. Cody crouched and took up a defensive position.

The sudden thunder of a gun near at hand caused Cody to flinch, Ned Pierce to spin angrily toward the door to the barn where Walt Donovan stood, the Colt in his hand trailing smoke.

'Knock it off, Ned,' the Triangle foreman said. 'That's not the way we welcome men to this ranch, and you know it.'

'He's a Stanton man,' Ned said in a fury of frustration.

'You don't know that. For myself, I doubt it.'

Ned Pierce just stood, fists still bunched, glowering at Donovan, whose face was still but rigidly set. Behind both men Joe Rowland walked to the barn door and went out, entering a minute later, leading Donovan's sorrel horse. The man was unwavering in his duties. Pierce seemed to have much he wanted to say, but he turned away from Cody in disgust, retrieved his hat and stormed out of the barn.

'What was that about?' the mustached Donovan asked.

'Nothing that I could tell,' Cody answered.

'As usual,' Donovan said bitterly. He glanced at Charlie Tuttle. 'You know this man, do you?'

Charlie nodded. 'We rode together for three years up on Domino. I was just offering to show Cody around and introduce him to some of the boys.'

'Do that. First he'd better meet the boss to make it official.' Donovan removed his hat and wiped back his salt-and-pepper hair. He told Cody seriously, 'When Ned takes a disliking to a man it sticks to him like a burr. I can't always be around to keep you out of trouble.'

'I wouldn't expect you to be,' Cody said.

Donovan looked the younger man over and nodded with apparent satisfaction. 'You'd better come along with me to the big house,' the Triangle foreman said.

Joe Rowland spoke up. Smiling, he asked, 'Walt, what would you say to letting me have the kid to help me out for a day or two? He's still a little banged up, and I could use some extra help.'

Donovan again eyed Cody, who appeared exhausted. His pant leg was stained with blood from the knocks he had taken. 'It's all right with me,' Donovan said with a shrug. 'Feel like swamping out the horse stalls tomorrow, Cody?'

'So long as it's work it suits me,' Cody Hawk answered, meaning it. This was no time to be particular, and a day spent with the cheerful Joe Rowland was preferable to many alternatives he could think of.

'You can have him then, Joe,' Donovan said. 'Depending on what the boss says, of course.'

There were lights on front and rear as they walked across the yard toward the big house. Someone was singing softly in the back of the house. A cook? Walt Donovan walked up the front steps as if he owned the place, Cody Hawk trailing behind. He was slightly apprehensive but Donovan seemed to be on his side. If the boss did not choose to hire him, he supposed he could try buying a horse from Triangle and hit the road again. It was still damnably cold out and he was not in the best shape. He did not wish to travel the long trails again, not so soon. But, since that was the worst that could happen, he removed his hat and followed Donovan into the neat house without expectations, but with quiet hope.

There was a braided rug in the entranceway and it muffled their bootsteps as they moved into the main room of the house, where a fire burned brightly in a white stone fireplace. The woman standing with her back to the fireplace was an astonishing sight to a rough country man like Cody Hawk. Around the age of twenty-five, she was not tall, but gave the impression of being of stature. Her eyes were a pale blue, dancing now with firelight. She wore a long white dress with a black sash tied to a bow in the back. Her little boots were the same blue as her eyes. Her dark hair was done up in an intricate fashion which nevertheless seemed loose and casual.

'This is Jewel Frazier,' Walt said by way of introduction. 'Jewel, this is Cody Hawk. Is your father around?'

'Is this about hiring on?' Jewel Frazier asked.

'Yes, it is.'

'Well, then,' the woman said with a small sigh, 'I suppose you will have to talk to my father. I'll send Remo upstairs.'

'No need for that,' a deep masculine voice said. 'I'm here, as you can see.'

The man who had to be the owner of the Triangle stood on the landing of the carpeted inside stairs. He wore a pearl-gray suit, gold vest and red cravat with a gold stickpin. He had once been handsome, Cody thought. Now his face had folded slightly at the jowls, and his shock of hair had gone completely white.

'Mr Frazier,' Donovan said with some warmth. 'It's good to see you again.'

The man worked his once-powerful body down the stairs, using the banister with every step. Reaching the firelit room, he strode heavily toward Donovan and took his hand.

'Glad you came over, Walt. What can I do for you?'

'It's about this young man, Cody Hawk,' Walt said.

'What's he done?' Frazier demanded. His daughter, Jewel, formed a slightly exasperated face.

'Cody? Nothing at all. He just arrived today from Domino. Since, as you know, Domino doesn't retain many hands over the winter, Cody's looking for work here.'

'Do we have much work to do around the place?' Frazier asked, walking to the hearth to warm his thick hands.

'We still have a lot of strays over near the Stanton place that should be pushed home,' Donovan said. 'There's a need for some yard work. I think we'll have to repair the bunkhouse roof soon. Joe Rowland has asked me for some temporary help. He asked specially if he could have Cody Hawk for the job.'

'Good old Joe,' Frazier said. 'Always has a smile for you.' He paused and then looked at Cody again. 'But who is this young man, Walt?'

Now Jewel quit trying to hold in her frustration. 'For God's sake, Dad! This is Cody Hawk. Walt wants to hire him on.'

'Well . . .' the old man hesitated. 'If you know who he is and Walt recommends him, I suppose we can give him a chance.'

Jewel turned away with obvious irritation. Frazier seemingly had a little trouble with his memory these days. He stared vaguely at the fire, still seeming confused. 'Is this the year we're going to finish off those Stantons, do you think, Walt?'

'I'd like to see them gone as much as you, sir, but

outside of making war on them, it looks like they're here to stay.'

'Vermin is what they are,' Frazier said. 'Been poaching my beeves for years.'

'That's why we're going to patrol the western range and start pushing those cows home,' Walt said patiently.

'That's a good idea, Walt! If you need extra men to get that done, we'll hire a few.'

'Yes, sir.'

Frazier looked blankly at Cody Hawk as if he had already forgotten who he could be and then turned to walk off in the direction of what had to be the kitchen.

'He's having one of his bad days,' Jewel Frazier apologized. 'This morning he mistook me for my mother.'

It seemed to Cody that Walt and Jewel Frazier wanted to have a longer, private conversation about the affairs of Triangle, and so he excused himself and went out into the cool of night. Well, he had been hired on – he supposed, from Frazier's vague comments. All he wanted now was a bite to eat and a bunk he could stretch out on to rest his injured leg. He limped toward the barn again. Charlie might still be waiting for him. He and Charlie also needed to have a private conversation soon. There was the little matter of $3,800 dollars in lost or stolen, gambled-away-and-murdered-for gold to discuss.

It was a clear bright morning, and it was startling to Cody Hawk's eyes. He lay still on his bunk for a long

time, organizing his memories. Charlie had brought
him over here from the barn the night before and a
man named Figaro or Figg, who seemed to be in
charge of the place, assigned a bunk to Cody. He had
met a few other hands, but could not remember their
names this morning. He had been given a bowl of
white beans and bacon, which he devoured more than
eagerly. He had slept as soundly as a dead man until
dawn.

Now men were up and moving around, joking and
grumbling. The bunkhouse had grown chill overnight,
but someone had started a fresh fire in the iron stove
which was set in the middle of the floor. Breakfast, it
seemed, had been served and devoured while Cody
slept. He sat up and swung his legs to the floor; a
sudden fierce pain in his knee reminded him of the
rough trail they had traveled. Wincing, he rubbed at
the calf of his leg, trying to lessen the pain in his knee.
It did no good at all.

'That's why we let you sleep,' the man Cody knew as
Figg said, appearing with a white tin bowl, a clean towel
and a roll of bandages. 'Charlie said you were pretty
banged up. It's a good thing you'll be working with Joe
Rowland the next few days and don't have to go riding
this morning.'

It was, and Cody wondered if that was the reason the
stableman had asked Walt Donovan for a man to help
him out.

'Let me see,' Figg, a hollow-cheeked, thinly bearded
man said, squatting down in front of Cody. 'Got to wash
it off first. I've got some carbolic poured into the water

88

in this pan.' He began wiping Cody's scabbed knee, dabbing lightly at the encrusted injury. 'Get shot there, did you?'

'No,' Cody said with a grimace as the carbolic acid met raw flesh, 'I did it to myself, trying to find out how fast a man could run into a tree in the dark.'

Figg looked up from his work with a smile. 'Someone chasing you, was there?'

'Most of the Stantons, it seemed. I know there were a lot of bullets flying.'

'They're a nasty bunch,' Figg commented. 'You know, Cody, I hate to tell you this, but you see this flap of hide peeled off your kneecap? I'm afraid I'm going to have to sew it back on or it won't heal proper.'

By the time Cody reached the barn, he knew he was late for work. Figg had taken his time sewing up Cody's wounded knee, taping up his sprained ankle. Then they shared coffee from the new pot Figg had boiled for the night-herders who were due in soon. His tardiness did not seem to bother the cheerful Joe Rowland.

'Are you up to a day's work?' Joe asked with a concerned glance.

'I think so. We'll find out.' Cody's leg was stiffer, more awkward than ever, but Figg had promised him that it would now heal quickly and properly.

'Yeah, old Figg knows what he's doing with scrapes and broken bones,' Joe Rowland said, handing Cody a rake and shovel he would need for his morning's work.

'For a while I was afraid they might set me to work

up on the bunkhouse roof. If you hadn't asked Walt for me . . .'

Joe's grin broadened and he shook his head. 'Walt's been telling the boss for years that he was going to need men to fix the bunkhouse roof – mostly when he wants to hire someone new. It's never gotten done yet.'

'Mr Frazier never notices?'

'Cody, you met Ernest Frazier – does he seem to you to be the type of man who notices much these days?'

'I guess not,' Cody said, taking the rake and wide shovel from Joe's hands.

'Not that he was always that way!' Joe said. 'Ernest Frazier was a fire-breathing, get-things-done type of man when I first reached Triangle. Men jumped when he spoke, I can tell you.'

'What happened to him?' Cody asked.

'Nothing. He was born, Cody. And we all know where that leads in the end.'

'Yes. I don't like to think about that much.'

'Nobody does. No, Ernest Frazier simply got old. Triangle goes on all the same. It's an awful burden on that young woman.'

'Jewel?'

Joe nodded. 'I didn't know you'd met her too.'

'I did. She seemed just a little nervous. But I suppose Walt Donovan handles most thing.'

'Walt tries. I don't know how much Jewel trusts him with – not after the last foreman.'

'What happened?'

'It's been a few years now,' Joe answered. 'I don't

know if it's even important any more.'

That ended that conversation. Cody limped along to the end of the horse stalls to start his work. He paused to pat Hungry, but the burro seemed utterly indifferent to his attentions. The skies had been nearly clear on this morning; a light breeze stirred. The doors to the barn were wide open, but still the interior of the barn was pretty rank.

Well, Cody thought, that's why they hired me. At least he had a job and a cot to return to when he was finished.

He hadn't seen Charlie Tuttle this morning. Figg told him that he was out helping the yard man, though there wasn't a lot Charlie could do with that injured arm of his. Figg had judged the bullet wound to be a 'Clean hole right on through. I packed it with sulfa powder. Charlie should be fine in no time – at least as soon as your leg is healed.'

Then the two would be ready to ride again in another week or so. But Cody was not so sure he wanted to leave Triangle, not when he had just arrived. As he had told both Charlie and Wayne more than once, he liked the idea of having steady work. Both of the older men had told him to make the best of the opportunity that had fallen into their laps – get off the range – but Cody was not so sure. If he had something else he wanted to do, but he did not. He was happy with what he had. Why spend his money on another place to shelter him when he had one here for free? One day he might feel different about things, but not now.

Charlie had been more than a little anxious about the money, and in the darkness last night, Cody told Charlie where he had hidden it. 'That's fine, kid,' Charlie had said, putting a hand on Cody's shoulder. 'Are you sure you can find it again?'

'Positive,' Cody reassured him.

'All right then, we're all set. As soon as my arm feels better and you're healed up, we'll maybe ride to Baxter.'

'Baxter?'

'It's the nearest town. You forget, Cody, I've worked on Triangle before, I've ridden into Baxter, it's a little more than ten miles south of here. A good place to winter up.'

'I'm not sure I'll be wanting to go,' Cody said.

'Well, you think about it, kid. You can afford it. If you decide not to go, we'll split the coin and I'll go on alone, though I'd rather you rode with me.'

Around noon Joe summoned Cody from the back of the barn. He had set up a trestle-table using a plank and a couple of barrels. There was a platter full of beef sandwiches and bowls of beans with bacon. Cody had already made the acquaintance of those beans the night before, but he had no qualms about revisiting them. As they ate they talked of little and nothing. Cody was halfway through his second sandwich when the man appeared in the doorway, blacking out the easy good feeling of the small dinner.

'Damn horse threw a shoe!' Ned Pierce half-shouted, indicating the sorrel he had been riding. 'I thought I told you to take care of that, Joe.'

'You did, and I did,' Joe answered, looking slightly uneasy now. 'I'll see to that right away.'

'In the meantime, I'm supposed to walk while I wait for you?' Pierce said gruffly.

Joe waved a hand along the aisle of stabled horses. 'Take any one you like, Pierce.'

'Any one that has all four shoes tacked on properly will do me,' the angry man said, stalking along the aisle between the horses.

When he went out a few minutes later, leading the pinto that had been offered to Cody the previous night, Joe was intently studying the right-hind shoe on the sorrel. When Ned Pierce had exited the horse barn, Joe dropped the sorrel's foot and returned to the table.

'It'll wait,' Joe muttered. Then he recovered his sandwich and his smile.

'He's never sunny, is he?' Cody said.

Joe sighed, putting his half-eaten sandwich down. 'No,' he agreed, 'he isn't. But you have to understand, Cody – Ned Pierce wasn't always like this. He used to be Ernest Frazier's golden boy. He was Triangle ranch manager and, a lot of people suspect, the intended husband of Jewel Frazier.'

'It sounds as if he had it made,' Cody commented. 'What happened to him?'

'Too much drinking had something to do with it. And he gambled pretty heavy. But these didn't matter to Mr Frazier, who was a bit of a hell-raiser himself in his day.

'No, Cody, what pulled the roof in on him was the

93

day he rode back in after having lost almost four thousand dollars of Triangle's money.'

# EIGHT

Cody Hawk just stared at Joe Rowland. He was not sure he had heard the stableman correctly. 'You say that Ned Pierce lost four thousand dollars?'

'Lost in the sense that he was robbed, or so he tells it. It was like this,' Joe told Cody, looking as serious as Cody had seen him. 'Do you know that army outpost up along the Saginaw?'

'Never seen it, but I've heard there's one there.'

'Well, the army contracted for beef and Frazier sent Ned Pierce up that way with a trail herd of five hundred steers. We didn't figure they would all make it, that mountain country being as rough as it is. Frazier thought they'd be lucky to get through without major losses.'

'He sent the ranch manager along with the herd, not Donovan the foreman?'

'Donovan hadn't even come on the scene yet, Cody. Being ranch manager was mostly just a fancy title; Ernest Frazier was his own ranch manager. Ned, no matter his faults, knows stock. He was the man to head the trail drive.'

'Something happened?'

'You bet something happened. Oh, the herd got through all right with only eighty beeves lost along the trail. Some of the crew demanded to be paid off at the trail head. I guess Ned was a little rough on them. Winter was settling in, anyway, and the boys were restless. A few of them even went to work for Domino. The rest scattered or laid up in McCormack for the winter. Whatever Ned had done along the way, he had made himself unpopular.'

'I remember a few Triangle boys riding onto Domino at that time, but there was heavy weather settling in and Domino doesn't take on new men that time of year. I think a few did manage to stay around.'

'In the end,' Joe went on, 'there was only Ned and the wrangler, Billy Post, to ride back to Triangle with the proceeds from the sale. Along the way they were set upon by robbers – Ned suspected that they were the Stantons. Billy Post was shot and Ned was left to travel on, the army gold gone.

'It snowed early and heavy that year in the mountains, and Ned was a month making his way back – without the crew, without the money. Ernest Frazier listened to Ned's tale. He didn't get mad. He knows these things can happen, but he had needed that money. His cash reserves were getting low and he had a ranch to run.

'He never said anything to Ned, but one day Walt Donovan showed up – Frazier had known him from their ranching days in Texas – and he was immediately named foreman, replacing Ned Pierce.'

'A hard pill for Pierce to swallow,' Cody said, not with any real sympathy because it seemed that Ned Pierce was a liar. Cody thought he knew where that money had gotten to. Oddly enough it had now finally found its way back to Triangle.

'Yes,' Joe agreed. He stretched his arms and rose, indicating that the dinner hour was over. 'What's eating at him most, I think, is that after that happened, Jewel wouldn't give Ned the time of day. And when Walt showed up, she shifted her attentions to him.'

'I see,' Cody said. 'Does Pierce still blame the Stantons for all of it – robbing him and causing him to lose his position and Jewel?'

'Does he not!' Joe said, laughing. 'None of his hatred for them has anything to do with the pilfering of a few cows. Ned had lived on a satin pillow on Triangle. A good job, his prospects high for marrying Frazier's daughter and heir.'

So Ned had stuck to his fictional account long enough for him to believe it himself. Cody was convinced that Ned, a known gambler, had stopped along the trail during a storm and decided to play some cards with a lonely trapper, losing the army payment. Knowing what he had done, what he was going to lose if he came back to Triangle empty-handed, he had thought things over and turned around on the trail to take care of things the only way he could – killing the trapper. What had happened to his trail partner, the wrangler Billy Post, he could not guess. But the Stantons had had nothing to do with it.

For one thing they didn't even own any horses. What did they do, walk up into the mountains in winter and wait for a man they had no way of knowing was about to pass carrying all that money? The idea was absurd. The whole story obviously a fabrication so that Ned would not have to return to Triangle and tell the truth – he had gambled away Frazier's money – and that he had killed a man but could not recover the money. The poverty-stricken, unlikable Stantons were ready scapegoats.

'What are you thinking, Cody?' Joe Rowland asked as he watched Cody return to his work with rake and shovel along the horse stalls. 'It seems your thoughts are far away.'

'I was just thinking that Ned Pierce spreads around more of this stuff than anyone.'

Joe smiled, whether he understood Cody's meaning or not, and got back to his own job, fixing a new horseshoe to Ned Pierce's sorrel.

An hour or so on, a small dark man Cody had not seen before entered the barn, looked around hesitantly and then made his way to where Joe was just putting his farrier's gear away. Joe greeted the man with a smile, nodded a few times and then pointed out Cody Hawk. The little man slipped away, wagging his head, and Joe came over to where Cody stood.

'You're wanted over at the big house,' Joe said.

'Me? Whatever for?'

'I wouldn't know, Cody. But you'd better put your tools up and get on over there. They want you to come to the back door.'

'Maybe I'll be washing some dishes or peeling potatoes,' Cody said. *Maybe Ned Pierce has already gotten me fired,* was what he was thinking.

There was nothing for it. With a smile that was less than relaxed, Cody put his tools aside, rolled down his sleeves and started out into the cool, bright day to make his way across the yard toward the back of the house. One of the yellow yard dogs sat watching him from the shade of an oak, its head cocked to one side curiously.

Removing his hat, Cody knocked cautiously at the half-screened back door. He could smell spicy food being prepared inside. It took a second series of knocks to bring the small dark man to the door, and he swung it open for Cody. He had a wooden spoon in his hand and he pointed with this toward an interior door across the spotless kitchen.

The little man returned to his work and Cody continued, warily. What was it that they wanted of him? His constant thought was that they had reconsidered and that he was now gong to be told that he was fired off the job.

He opened the inner door and found himself on the far side of the great room with the fireplace. She was seated on the end of the black-and-white cowhide sofa, her feet drawn up beneath her.

Jewel Frazier glanced up from what she was doing – toying with a small nickel-plated revolver – and motioned Cody to approach her. He did so, hat still in his hands, still moving with a limp. The girl with the blue eyes looked up, measured him, and offered him a seat. Cody's stiff leg prompted him to remain standing. He explained this to Jewel, who no longer wore her dress and little blue boots, but standard riding gear. Sturdy jodhpur boots, black jeans and a plain white blouse. Her hair was worn loose on this day, and it flowed in dark cascades around her shoulders and breast.

'Your father wanted to see me,' Cody began, trying to keep his eyes off Jewel. It was difficult – she was simply beautiful.

'No. I'm the one who sent for you,' Jewel said. She snapped shut the cylinder of the little .32 pistol she had been toying with. 'Father's up taking one of the several naps he takes every day before bedtime.'

'He's not well?' Cody offered.

'He's old,' Jewel shrugged. 'Wore himself out building Triangle.'

'It can be a struggle.' Cody knew.

Jewel answered him sharply. 'I don't intend to let that happen to me,' she announced. Cody had no answer to make. She rose to her feet, pistol in hand. 'Sit down, will you? You're making me nervous.'

Cody complied, lowering himself uncomfortably onto a maroon leather chair. Jewel Frazier was starting to make *him* nervous, the way she waved that pistol around as she spoke. Her eyes were bright with some unfathomable emotion. Cody waited for her to get to her point, whatever that might be.

'Father thinks he has provided me with everything I need,' she said, stopping directly in front of Cody, legs slightly spread, pistol still dangling from her hand.

Cody seemed expected to reply. He looked around the beautiful house and said:

'You have a fine home, a cook, any horse you wish, steady income. . . .'

'And that might be enough for any man, Cody Hawk,' she said, bending forward at the waist toward him, 'but I am not a man!'

Cody, who had noticed that, could only think to nod agreement.

'I'll tell you a story, Cody Hawk. It won't seem important to you because you are a man. When I was twelve I decided that I wanted to make my next birthday party on Triangle a big one. I would invite everyone for miles around to attend. Dancing, Japanese lanterns strung in the trees out front. Father took me all the way to Baxter, where I ordered a certain party dress from their mail-order catalogue. It was to come all the way from Chicago. You know how slow mail and freight move out here.' Cody nodded vaguely. Was he supposed to say something? Jewel continued, waving the gun around wildly as she spoke.

'After months and months of waiting, the dress finally arrived a week before the planned party. I was so thrilled – until I tried it on. In the months previous, Cody Hawk, I had filled out so much here and there that the dress was impossibly tight. My thirteenth birthday party was ruined!'

Again Cody could think of nothing to say. He murmured a barely audible, 'Too bad,' which Jewel seemed not to hear. Her mouth had grown as petulant as a thirteen-year-old's.

101

'That's the way everything is out here,' she said, recovering herself. 'This is no place for a woman to live. I want to be able to buy a new hat when I see it, get a dress from a shop window that fits, go to dances with men who don't wear cowboy boots, to speak to people who know about something beside horses and cattle. Now! Before I grow older.'

'I can understand that,' said Cody, who thought that he could. He still didn't know what this had to do with him or why Jewel had chosen to talk to him about childhood disappointments. He didn't have to wait long to find out. Again she drew herself up in front of him and announced:

'I have been speaking with Ned Pierce.'

So that was it. Cody felt his stomach constrict a little. The woman with the gun in her delicate little hand went on:

'Three years ago when Ned was still foreman of Triangle, he and I decided to get out of here – Ned wants what I want – a piece of civilization where everything doesn't stink of manure.'

And where he could gamble and drink at will with a beautiful woman waiting for him at home. A woman who also happened to be an heiress. No fool, Ned Pierce.

'We had planned everything out carefully. After the cattle herd was delivered to the army post up along the Saginaw, we were going to chuck it in and head off together for Baxter. I was already packing before the herd left Triangle. Then,' she said with a long, elaborate sigh, 'the fool got himself robbed along the trail.'

'He couldn't help that,' Cody said.

Jewel came nearer still and leaned over Cody. 'He told us that it was the Stantons who did it.'

Cody felt like answering that you could tell that by the palatial way the Stantons lived, but thought it better to keep his mouth shut. As if reading his mind, Jewel said, 'Of course they never spent a penny of it; that would have been giving themselves away. So the money, four thousand dollars, is all still together.'

'Is it?'

'Yes.' Jewel's eyes blazed, her nostrils flared with excitement. 'And Ned told me who has it now.'

'Who?' Cody asked weakly. Jewel's little nickel-plated revolver continued in evidence.

'Who?' she asked almost coyly. 'A man who has just arrived from the Stanton place, leading their burro carrying heavy saddle-bags.'

Cody tried laughing. 'Me? How could I have gotten the money? Where would I be going with it?'

'Ned thinks that either you killed them and took the money or you're with them, maybe transferring it to a bank in Baxter.'

'Why would I stop here!' Cody protested. It was hard to deny something that was so close to the truth, and his voice seemed to betray him.

'You were wounded, you had no choice,' Jewel said simply. She spun her back toward Cody and walked away a few steps, her boot heels clicking against the wooden floor. 'Cody, I would let any man who had that much money escort me to Baxter. It's mine, you know.'

'It's Triangle's,' Cody said realizing only after he had

spoken that this was dangerously close to being an admission of sorts. He was not clever at parlor games, and he felt he was losing this one.

'Do you think my father needs more money? He doesn't even remember that it is gone, nor would he have an idea what to do with it. To me it is of crucial importance. I have to get off this ranch or lose my mind!'

Cody wondered if she had not already done that. The pistol continued to wave around the room; Jewel's eyes continued to carry fire. 'You and I could travel to Baxter, Cody,' she said softly, again approaching him.

'I think you're mistaken about things, Jewel,' he said. 'What about your father, the ranch, everything you'd be leaving behind?'

'Father has no needs but his bed and meals, and we have Remo to take care of him.' She nodded toward the kitchen, where the dark man worked. 'As for losing anything, I shan't. I am the only heir to Triangle. Baxter isn't that far away. I can always be notified if something happens. Walt Donovan is here to take care of day-to-day matters, and Walt is a good man.'

Cody could only stare at the woman. He supposed that in her own mind she was thinking of doing nothing wrong, and maybe she wasn't. The ranch would soon be hers, the money was Triangle's. Her father seemed to need little these days. Still. . . .

Cody rose abruptly, or as abruptly as he could on his stiff leg. He said, 'I'm sorry, Miss Frazier, I can't really see how I can help you. Everyone seems to be assuming I know a lot more than I do.'

Jewel's eyes said *liar*, but she only nodded as if with sadness and finally put the pistol away. 'You think it over, Cody Hawk. I mean you no harm and I can be an entertaining companion for the right man.' She moved toward him but he backed up a few steps defensively.

Cody had had enough. In another few minutes, she'd have him convinced that the money was rightfully hers and that she needed Cody as her hero and protector. Cody had never thought of himself as a clever man, but he did not like the way this was trending. He did not need to drink the poison to the dregs to realize that it was leaving a bad taste in his mouth. Jewel's blue eyes watched Cody as he made his way toward the front door of the house. It was with relief that he opened it and stepped outside.

From within he heard Ernest Frazier calling. 'Who was that? Did someone just leave?'

'It was Cody Hawk,' he heard Jewel answer in a narrow voice.

'Who? Have I met him?' Frazier wanted to know.

Cody closed the door softly and continued on his way.

Walking back toward the barn, the wind from the north urging him along his way, Cody turned matters over in his mind. He came to a solitary conclusion: Charlie had been right. They should have avoided Triangle all together. There was trouble brewing here from all directions.

Joe Rowland was inside the barn. He seemed to have just snatched up a rake to mimic working as if he feared being caught idle. There was a welcoming smile on his face.

'How did things go with the boss?' Joe asked.

'Fine,' Cody lied. 'I'm still working here.'

'Good. I knew it couldn't be much. Say, Cody, the place looks pretty clean now; I have another job for you.'

'I know, you want me to repair the bunkhouse roof.'

Joe laughed at what seemed to be a standard joke around Triangle. 'No, what happened is this – do you know Brent Preston?'

'Not by name.'

'He said he brought you into the ranch yesterday on his hay wagon.'

'Oh, him, yes. We never got around to exchanging names.'

'When Ned came back to pick up his sorrel, he spotted Brent and told him he needed another man with him on western patrol. He thinks he might run into the Stantons out there since our beeves haven't all been rounded up and driven in yet. Anyway, upshot is that Brent went off with Ned Pierce, leaving no one to fork winter feed to the cattle.

'Ned said to send Charlie Tuttle out to do it,' Joe finished. He was not smiling now.

'A man with only one good arm!' Cody said, flaring up.

'I know. It's a bum deal for Charlie, and I said as much to Ned. Ned said just to do as he said. It wasn't his fault if Triangle seemed to be making a habit of hiring on cripples.'

106

'Nice guy,' Cody mumbled.

Joe's face had brightened again. He told Cody, 'Like I said, the barn looks pretty well swamped out now. It's probably best for all concerned if you ride on out and help Charlie Tuttle pitch hay . . . if you're up to the job yourself.'

'All right,' Cody agreed. 'Where will I find him?'

'Right near where Brent picked you up yesterday – just look around. A hay wagon isn't hard to spot.'

'Mind if I take the gray horse?' Cody asked, nodding toward Wayne Tucker's horse, which seemed well rested now, eager to travel.

'It's not a Triangle pony,' Joe answered. 'It makes no difference to me.'

Cody had ridden Wayne's horse before, but still it shied when he approached it with its bridle and bit. Cody took a few moments to pause and remember the sharp-featured, sometimes abrasive Wayne Tucker who had been his second 'father', then he prepared the horse for riding, and with the sun still high in the wide sky, trailed out to find Charlie Tuttle.

He found his friend within fifteen minutes. Standing in the back of the hay wagon, awkwardly trying to fork hay to the gathered steers using only his good right arm, he was red-faced. His lips moved with a series of silent curses.

'Who did you get mad?' Cody asked Charlie cheerfully as he reined up behind the wagon.

'Who else?' Charlie answered, 'but I don't know how.' He straightened to remove his hat and wipe the sweat from his brow. The cattle around the wagon lowed as with impatience. Charlie nearly shouted: 'I'm forking as fast as I can!'

He looked down at Cody, who was tying the gray horse to the back of the wagon. 'I'm working my fool head off while some of us go trotting around on their friend's horse. There's no justice.'

'I'm a favored child of the gods,' Cody said, clambering up onto the bed of the wagon. 'Really, I was sent out to help you.'

'None too soon,' Charlie complained. 'I don't know how I'm supposed to get my arm healed up working like this.'

Cody took the pitchfork from Charlie's hand. After distributing some hay to the waiting cattle, he told Charlie, 'You know, I've been doing some thinking.' Cody tipped his hat back and leaned on the fork for a moment. 'You may have been right, Charlie. It may be that it isn't the best idea for me to plan on staying around Triangle.'

'You're serious?' Charlie Tuttle asked.

'Yes, I am. We don't need to – you're right about that. And something happened to me today that is almost unbelievable. Over at the big house,' he went on as Charlie's eyes shifted and squinted into the western light. 'You see. . . .'

'Whatever it was,' Charlie said, 'I'll bet you it wasn't as unbelievable as what's about to happen.'

Cody had no idea what Charlie was talking about. Walking forward in the wagon, he stood beside the stake rails and watched the small figure approaching them in the distance.

It was difficult to be certain from so far away, but it seemed that the shaggy white horse heading their way was being ridden by Lonnie Stanton.

# NINE

'Now what?' Cody Hawk muttered.

'Now we clear out of this country,' Charlie Tuttle said. For as the horse drew nearer they could see for certain that it was Lonnie Stanton on the plow horse's back, riding with no saddle, with her Winchester rifle across the shaggy animal's withers.

'I don't know what happened to you earlier, Cody, but it's time we recover that gold and line out of here.'

'We've got to talk to the girl first, to see what she wants.'

'*You* talk to her,' Charlie said, grabbing the pitchfork, 'I've had my fill of talking to Stantons.'

'All right,' Cody agreed. It was only right to see what she wanted. The girl had ridden all this way at some risk to herself. And she had obviously already recognized them.

He slipped from the hay wagon, tugged free the slipknot securing the reins of the gray and led the horse forward to meet Lonnie. Halfway to her he halted and waited for her to approach on the slow-moving plow horse. She was wearing a blue skirt, blue blouse and white straw hat, which Cody took to be her best wear. The face of the small woman was determined, her eyes set.

'I'm more than a little surprised to see you, Lonnie,' Cody said as she halted the horse. 'What can I do for you?'

'I come for my money,' the girl said forcefully.

'I don't think I understand.'

'Oh, I think you do – or you should. I come for my fortune, Uncle Morris's gold! I want it.' Her small chin trembled as she said this. The girl was excited, overly so. Cody noticed that she kept turning her head, looking behind her as if expecting someone to arrive.

'Let's find another place to talk,' Cody said, mounting the gray. 'You never can tell who might come along. You are on Triangle land, you know.'

' 'Course I know! What do you take me for?'

A very frightened young woman, was the answer to that, but Cody did not say so. Instead he suggested, 'I know a hidden place. Let me just tell my friend.'

'If you think you're going to take me off somewhere and kill me, remember I've still got my rifle and I know how to use it.'

'I know you do,' was Cody's reply. He inclined his head and started the gray horse on its way. He had noticed a canyon, really no more than a notch in the low ridge running parallel to the valley floor, and he guided the gray in that direction, turning his head now and then to make sure that Lonnie was following. She

111

was, her expression as bright as a person being led to execution.

Inside the stony notch there was some poor grass and a thicket of sumac, little else, except for a range steer which had somehow found its way there and now watched them with dull eyes as it tugged at the yellow grass.

Cody swung down near a scramble of fallen rocks and seated himself, inviting Lonnie to join him. The girl's eyes were wary, the rifle firmly in her grip as she slipped from the white horse's back and joined him.

'Now, then,' Cody began, 'what is it that you want from me?'

'I've told you. My fortune, the one my Uncle Morris intended for me. You've stolen it.'

'I've never even laid eyes on your Uncle Morris,' Cody said. *Not while he was alive.* His voice sounded oddly uncertain to his own ears. Lonnie Stanton must have heard the lack of conviction in his words as well. The girl, sitting on a rock with her legs tucked under her blue skirt, rifle across her knees, frowned even more heavily.

Would she shoot? Had it been a terrible mistake to bring her to this secluded place?

He tried again. 'Tell me about this missing treasure and why you think I would know anything about it.'

'All right,' she agreed. She had removed her wide straw hat and the breeze was strong enough to drift and twist her long hair even in this sheltered place. That was not a good sign; Cody glanced northward to see dark storm clouds beginning to gather over the mountains. It would snow again and soon. 'I will tell you what happened,' Lonnie said after a thoughtful moment of silence. Cody noticed that her rough mountain accent had faded.

'This may take a while,' Lonnie said. Cody nodded in response and waited. The steer had moved over to graze nearly in front of them like some curious eavesdropper. The two horses shared the meager grass with the cow. Lonnie took a deep, slow breath and told Cody:

'A couple of years ago we were digging in for a long, cold winter. I got to thinking about my Uncle Morris, who was alone in the far high mountains. He knew how to survive harsh weather, that was certain, but he lived mostly off wild meat and gather.'

'I liked my Uncle Morris. He never harmed anyone. Mostly he just wanted to be left alone. When I was little he used to bring me things like a fox's tail or a rabbit skin…' Lonnie's eyes drifted briefly away, perhaps he was remembering the pleasure those small gifts had given her. She sat up rigidly, still not meeting Cody's eyes. She wiped strands of wind-drifted hair from her eyes.

'Anyway, I decided on my own to visit my Uncle Morris before the snows got any worse. I took items from our larder – I would have gotten in trouble over that. But we had plenty that year. I took two burlap bags and loaded them with sugar, coffee, corn meal, beans and wheat flour – a few other things I can't recall – and I loaded them onto Daisy's back. That's the burro's name,' she said at Cody's questioning look.

113

'The weather was mild when I started out, but by the time I reached Rios Canyon it had begun to snow again. I could see that it had fallen heavily earlier. I had to put on my snow shoes to make it the last mile or so to Uncle Morris's cabin.

'He was surprised and happy to see me, but there was a worried look on his face. He asked me if I had passed anybody on the way up. I hadn't seen a soul. He muttered, "I wonder if the bastard's still around, then?"

'I asked him who he meant, but he just shook his head. Then he began to try to hurry me away instead of having a little visit. He said it was going to snow again and he didn't want me trapped up there, but that wasn't it, I knew. He was worried that whoever he was talking about might come back.

'That's when he told me about the fortune. Uncle Morris said he would see that it got to me soon so that I could go off and have the sort of life a young girl needs. But I was not to tell Emil or even my mother about it.'

'Did he say how he could have come by a fortune way up there?' Cody asked.

'No. He was very mysterious about that, almost frightened to tell me, it seemed. But Uncle Morris was not a liar, and if he said he had a fortune, he had it.'

'I wonder why he didn't want you to tell the rest of your family?'

'Because they would take it away from me and use it for other things. Uncle Morris wanted me to be able to go away somewhere.'

'Is Emil Stanton your father?' Cody asked.

114

Lonnie shook her head, gave a little sigh and repositioned her legs. 'No. He took me in along with Mother. As for the boys, I get along well enough with Luke. He and I more or less grew up together. But Amos and Daltry. . .' She shuddered and it was not because the wind had grown cooler. 'Ever since I was little, they have been looking at me, or trying to.'

'I don't know what you mean,' Cody told her.

'Use your imagination,' Lonnie snapped.

'Oh,' Cody said, feeling like a fool.

'Uncle Morris knew all about that – I'd told him. He was the only one I trusted.'

'Your mother . . .'

'Every time I told her anything she'd run to Emil and tell him. She fears him and is afraid of losing him, both. She doesn't know how she'd survive if something happened to Emil.'

'I see,' Cody said, believing that he did. 'But to get back to the point: what makes you think I have Uncle Morris's fortune?'

'That bullet I spanked off your friend's saddle-bags for one thing!' Lonnie said with some excitement. 'That was on purpose, of course – I'm not that bad a shot, and I wouldn't be trying to injure a horse. And the way he – the one with the mustache . . .'

'Wayne,' Cody supplied.

'The way Wayne carried those saddle-bags and sheltered them around the house. I've never seen a man so concerned about his camp utensils, which is what he told us were in the bags.'

Cody had warned Wayne Tucker about that, but

115

Wayne had been more interested in protecting the gold than what the Stantons might think of him.

'Wayne might have been carrying something valuable,' Cody admitted, 'but what makes you think it was your Uncle Morris's treasure?'

'Where were you three riding in from? There's only one way to travel down those mountains to Rios Canyon. Did you happen by a cabin on your way?'

'If we did . . .' Cody began, but stopped before he trapped himself.

'I knew it,' Lonnie said with triumph. 'You found what Amos and Daltry never could.'

'How could they even know about it?'

'I let it slip one day when I was angry. I said that when I got my Uncle Morris's fortune, they'd all be sorry.' Lonnie waved a hand in the air. 'I hate anger. It can make a person say and do the stupidest things!'

Cody had to agree. 'What about the boys – Amos and Daltry – won't they be following you now, thinking you'll lead them to the treasure?'

'They have no horses. I took the only one.' She frowned thoughtfully. 'Although they were talking about ambushing some Triangle riders for their ponies.'

And that would start a range war. Cody knew that both Walt Donovan and Ned Pierce – who particularly hated the Stantons – were on the western range, rounding up Triangle strays. Things had gotten snarled up wildly, and it seemed matters could only get worse. He was certain now that Charlie was right. The two of them had to leave Triangle while they still could.

116

He glanced skyward again. The sky was an inky blue; the wind continued to build, as did the gathering storm clouds up along Rios Canyon. Of course the weather was not going to cooperate either. Muttering, Cody rose to his feet.

'Look, Lonnie,' Cody said seriously, 'it seems obvious that you can't go home and don't want to. You certainly can't stay around Triangle.' He thought briefly of Jewel Frazier. 'What do you intend to do, then?'

Lonnie Stanton rose and brushed her skirt with one hand. The other held firm to the Winchester.

'If you would have given me my fortune, I was planning on making my way to Baxter. Now . . .' she shook her head. 'I just don't know. That was as far as my thinking went.'

Her eyes were downcast. There was something so pitiful about this lost child-woman that Cody was prompted to make a gesture. He reached into his pocket where he had placed some of the stolen money in case of an emergency. Well, this was an emergency, if not his.

'I saved a little money while I was working for Domino,' Cody lied. Another lie; was it getting easier for him? He had told more of them recently than he had in his entire life. He placed three bright ten-dollar gold pieces in Lonnie's palm. She eyed them and Cody dubiously. 'Go on to Baxter before this storm settles in. Find a room for rent or check in at the hotel. Later maybe you can find work as a cook, a maid – who knows? You'll be better off than you were at Emil

Stanton's place.'

Lonnie shrugged an answer and pocketed the coins. She didn't believe Cody's explanation as to their origin, he thought.

'I guess that's all there is to do,' she said as she walked toward her shaggy white horse.

Alongside her, Cody asked, 'Are you sure Amos and Daltry aren't following you?'

'I'm sure,' Lonnie said, swinging up on the plow horse's back. 'But you know, Cody Hawk, someone else might have been. I couldn't make him out; he kept his distance. Or maybe I was imagining things. Who else could it have been, deliberately following me?'

Who else, indeed, except the mysterious, shadowy man whom Cody had noticed on more than one occasion, following him?

'Will I see you in Baxter?' Lonnie asked from her mounted position.

'What makes you think I'm going anywhere?' he demanded with faint truculence.

'Well, Cody Hawk, I think it's like this: you can no longer stay around this part of the country without something terrible happening to you, any more than I can.'

Cody would have argued with the girl, but there was no point to argue. Her conclusion was, unfortunately, quite accurate. He watched her ride away on the shaggy horse. She did not turn to wave, did not call a word of farewell. With no other business to occupy him at that moment, he mounted the gray horse and hied the feeding steer out of the notch to rejoin the herd.

'Your picnic over so soon?' a red-faced Charlie Tuttle greeted him.

Cody was scowling. 'Shut up. I'll tell you about it later, Charlie,' he said as the gray side stepped and turned as some of the cattle got too near its flanks. 'It's time to go.'

'That's what you were saying,' Charlie replied, mopping at his face with a blue bandanna.

'I mean now! We've got to be going, Charlie, while we've the chance.'

If they still had one at all.

'All right,' Charlie agreed, rightly reading the anxiety on Cody's face. He glanced at the skies. 'I'll tell anyone who asks that it was getting too bitter cold out here for a wounded man.'

'No one's going to say a thing to you. We won't be here. Turn the wagon and bring it in.'

'If we're leaving we'll need another horse.'

'Joe won't care if we saddle another horse, though I'd rather not take an animal with a Triangle brand. If need be, I'll buy one.'

'You be careful, Cody,' Charlie warned him. 'You be very careful about flashing any of that gold around. It could be a death warrant.'

By the time they reached the barn the skies were roofed over with blue-black clouds. These trembled before the rising wind as if eager to have their strength unleashed. The long grass was flattened, the trees shuddered in anticipation as the few leaves remaining on their branches tumbled away.

Cody helped Charlie put the hay wagon in its shed

after unharnessing the horses. As they walked to the barn a few stray snowflakes hit their shoulders and hats. It was not going to be a good night for riding.

'Just let me get my gear from the bunkhouse,' Charlie said, 'and we'll be on our way.'

'How much does that gear mean to you?' Cody asked. 'With the weather turning like it is, the boys from the range will be coming in. That means Donovan will be back. And Ned Pierce. I don't think we should stop for anything we don't need.'

Joe Rowland was not really surprised to see them come in so early, the weather being what it was. Cody told him what they needed. Explaining why they needed another saddle horse might have been difficult, but Joe was not there to ask questions. When a man needed a horse on Triangle, he was given one.

'How about the little pinto?' Joe suggested. 'Ned had it out already today, but that was only for a few hours while I was shoeing his sorrel.'

Cody told Joe that the little pinto would do fine. Cody switched his saddle to the pinto, since they had agreed beforehand that Charlie would ride Wayne Tucker's big gray horse.

Then, without further preparations, they exited the barn in time to see the range patrol riding in from the west. These were only shadows in the snow now. Probably, Cody thought, with the weather turning as it was they should have found a way to delay their departure, but doing so might have run them into some quite deadly problems.

Before leaving, Cody took one minute to pause and

tell Joe:

'The burro's name is Daisy.' Then they were gone, riding into the thick of the storm, away from Triangle and its riders.

It was not difficult to recover the stolen gold. Snow had lightly dusted the jumble of rocks, but not enough to conceal the small cleft where Cody had placed the saddle-bags. These were passed to Charlie to strap on behind his saddle, which he did with an expression of relief on his round face, even as he was looking around him with some anxiety in his eyes. They were so near to making their escape; they could not be discovered now.

As they rode out of the valley in the direction of Baxter town, following a trail Charlie knew from earlier years, the snow began to fall in earnest. A soft, enclosing blanket of white built around them. It would make travel more difficult, but it would also conceal them from any following men.

Once across the first row of low, flanking hills, the road ahead of them flattened out and lay in a generally straight line southward. Once, at the top of a rise, Charlie reined in and waited for Cody, who was trailing on the pinto.

'Ten miles,' Charlie said, lifting a gloved hand to point. 'If it weren't for the weather this would be a picnic.'

'We'll be in Baxter before full dark, then.'

'We should be, easily. If the storm lets us; if we don't run into any trouble. Cody,' the older man said, 'do you realize how many people are going to be on our heels?'

121

There were the Stanton brothers, possibly with Emil accompanying them, if they had managed to steal some Triangle horses, as Lonnie had told him was what they had in mind. Of course if Ned Pierce had further suspicions, stoked by the fact that the two had ridden out unannounced, he would be on their trail. With Jewel Frazier at his side? Who knew – the wild-eyed Jewel seemed capable of almost anything. Any number of Triangle men might follow along if Ned and Jewel accused the pair of stealing Triangle horses, especially if the Stantons had already angered them by descending to horse-stealing.

There was yet another man, though Cody had no idea who it could be: the mysterious man who had been following them down Rios Canyon on their way out of the mountains. The same man who had been trailing Lonnie? Whoever he was – if he was not only some product of their imaginations – he had not yet tried to take a shot at any of them, but that meant nothing. He might only have been waiting for the right moment.

'A few,' Cody answered Charlie after a long minute's reflection.

'I suppose we'll be all right once we get to Baxter and deposit the money in the bank.'

'At least we're off Triangle, and we have the money!' Cody said above the wind.

As the snow fell harder, Charlie said, 'Just tell me that we're not doing all of this for the sake of a girl, Cody.'

Cody laughed as they started on their way again. Charlie's remark was ridiculous.

Wasn't it?

The snow fell, the sky darkened still more and the wind pushed heavily at their backs as the horses plodded on across the miles of wasteland toward the small town in the unseen distance.

Where Lonnie Stanton waited.

# TEN

The wind had shifted, now blowing out of the west. It had not lessened, but seemed to be drifting the weight of the storm away from them. The snow fell more lightly, though with darkness descending the visibility was no better. The horses plodded on gamely although now and then Cody could feel the little pinto falter beneath him. Both horses had already had a full day's work. But there was not much farther to go, and soon the ponies would be rested and fed for their efforts.

Now as they seemed to be free of the wrath of the storm and away from following guns, Cody took the time to explain about his conversations with both Jewel Frazier and Lonnie Stanton.

'The way they were telling it, they both seem to have a claim to that money, Charlie. It's pretty obvious that it was Triangle money that Ned Pierce gambled away. Yet, if Uncle Morris won it honestly in that last card game, it was promised to her and should go to Lonnie.'

Charlie only grunted. It was obvious he believed the money belonged to the three men who had discovered its hiding-place. To Charlie it was a matter of salvage rights, the same as if they had recovered a sunken ship. Cody wasn't about to argue with him. Not at this point. He was still sifting the two women's opposing claims in his mind. One or both could be lying to him, saying anything to claim ownership of the gold. It was easier to credit Jewel Frazier's claim; more difficult to believe that she was honest.

'Somebody's got to be telling me the truth,' Cody said in frustration.

'You'd hope so,' Charlie responded. 'But then, they're both women.'

Cody sensed a long conversation about women's natures coming, and he wanted to avoid it. He actually found himself wishing that Wayne Tucker were still with them, to engage in his favorite sport of baiting Charlie. Honestly, though Cody could not explain it to himself, he missed the constant bickering between the two older men. Maybe Charlie, too, missed his old friend more than he was willing to admit. Cody could not be drawn into this sort of conversation. He had spent years avoiding the arguments when Charlie and Wayne started going at it.

The town of Baxter seemed to be growing no nearer. It might have been close enough to see under normal conditions, but wherever the town lay on the plains it was now only a small white collection of buildings lost in a white background.

It grew dark rapidly. The world went to Prussian blue and then to complete blackness. Without even starlight to guide them the travel became slow, plodding. The two men rode close together so as not to get separated in the black, stormy night. Charlie continued to speak.

'Nearly there,' he said in a hoarse whisper. He seemed very weary suddenly. Cody realized he had given Charlie's injury little thought. His arm must have been aching tremendously. 'I mean to find me a warm bed, eat some good food, talk to someone of the opposite sex, maybe drink a few beers and sit planning the rest of my life.

'With Wayne gone it's an even split now, kid. That's almost two thousand for each of us. You do whatever you want with your half – split it with the girl, give it all to her or to Jewel Frazier. I don't care. My half will carry me along for quite some time. When I have the time, I mean to look around for a little place. . . .'

That was when the night rang with sudden rifle fire. Charlie, in mid-sentence, was tossed from his horse as the gray bucked in panic. Charlie did not feel it when he landed crookedly against the snow-mantled earth. One of the bullets had taken the top of his skull off.

Cody spun, searching for his attackers, looking for muzzle flashes, but he saw nothing, heard nothing but the still-echoing gunfire. The night seemed as empty as ever. Two more rifle shots were let loose and Cody leaned low in the saddle, hooking the reins to the gray in his fingers. Then he heeled the pinto pony roughly and he was suddenly riding blind through the whirl and wash of the snowstorm in what he hoped was the direction of Baxter, leading Wayne Tucker's gray with its burden of gold.

The pinto ran as fast and far as it was capable. Cody

felt the pony begin to falter, to slow, and suddenly it halted, shuddering beneath him. The pinto would not move, no matter how Cody tried to urge it on.

The gray was a bigger, fresher horse, so Cody swung from the pinto's back and stepped into the gray's leather. He did not wish to leave the pinto behind, but there was little time for pity. Perhaps when it recovered it would be able to make its own way to Baxter. The knowledge that there were men out on this night with killing on their minds left little room in his thoughts to concern himself with animals. Charlie was dead, and he was unwilling to join him.

Cody rode on desperately through the storm, which would ease and then whip out in fury, opening a lane of vision only to slam it closed once again. He did not see anyone following him, but then how could he? They – whoever they were – had managed to catch up with Charlie and Cody unseen in the snowstorm once.

The strength of the big gray horse was beginning to flag. The wind was constant, the snow as heavy as it had ever been.

Topping a low rise, he came upon the huddled little town of Baxter spread out before him. He slowed the gray and walked it toward the town, half-turned in his saddle to watch for approaching riders. Maybe his attackers had no horses. Maybe they had struck from an ambush site they had chosen. It seemed unlikely, yet everything on this confused night seemed unlikely. Cody did not ponder it long. Shameful or not, his own safety was his only concern at the moment.

Baxter was like a frosted little village out of some

magazine illustrator's imagination at this late hour.
The town was laid out like a checkerboard, the streets
at right angles to each other. Lanterns blinked in only
a few dozen windows. The snow along the main street
was deep; very few horses were passing to trample it
down. The structures along the avenue cut the force of
the wind. Cody could not read the signs on the fronts
of the buildings he passed because of the snow clinging
to them, but the stable was not hard to find. Tall
double doors and a distinct smell marked it for what it
was. A lantern was burning inside. He could see its glow
through a greasy window. Even in this weather
someone would be tending the place.

The front doors being closed against the weather,
Cody tapped at the door on the side of a smaller structure attached to the side of the horse barn. A voice
called out, not cheerfully:

'What is it?'

'I've got a horse to put up.'

There was a pause, a grumble and the man called
out, 'Come around front.'

Cody led the weary gray to the double doors and
waited as a bolt was thrown and a door swung wide. 'I
was sleeping,' the stableman complained. He was
short, stocky with a chubby face and a nose which
almost disappeared into the flab of his cheeks. He wore
a denim jacket lined with sheepskin.

'Sounds like the thing to do on a night like this,'
Cody said. 'That's what I plan on doing myself.' He
slipped the saddle-bags from the gray and watched as
the man inspected the horse, running a hand along its

withers. He glanced then at the brand, which was Rafter T out of Wyoming, where Wayne Tucker had worked for many years. Cody found himself almost happy that he had not made it into town with the Triangle-branded pinto pony. Anonymity suddenly seemed prudent.

'You didn't show this horse much mercy, did you?' the stable hand growled, loosening the saddle cinches. His complaint was typical of many a man you ran across in stables who genuinely cared about their charges. Cody kept his answer light.

'Had to get in. I didn't think spending a night on the plains would do either of us much good.' The man gave a small grunt as he hoisted the saddle and tossed it over a stall railing; Cody decided to give the man a friendly stroke. 'I'm sure you'll have him good as new before I have to ride again. Folks say you're one of the best horse men around.'

'Prob'ly the best,' the man answered, likely believing it himself.

Cody asked about a hotel and was given directions. He slogged across the snow-covered street and up onto an awning-sheltered boardwalk, then traveled the three blocks to where an imposing – for this part of the country – yellow-brick building stood staunchly on the corner of intersecting streets, the light from within promising warmth and comfort.

The door opened silently on oiled brass hinges. Cody crossed the polished wooden floor still shedding snow though he had tried to brush the worst of it off before entering. A narrow man with small, dark,

earnest eyes stood behind the mahogany desk as if
eager to serve. Cody stepped up to the orderly counter
and placed the saddle-bags at his feet.

'Good evening, sir. Rotten weather tonight, isn't it?'

'Pretty harsh, yes. I hope you can find a room for
me.'

'Is upstairs all right with you?' Cody was asked.

'It doesn't matter to me so long as it has a bed and a
roof over it.'

Entering Wayne's name instead of his own in the
hotel register – there was no telling who might come
looking for him in this town – he noticed a familiar
name scrawled in a childish hand several lines above.
He looked to the clerk and asked:

'What room is Miss Lonnie Stanton in?'

The clerk shook his head slightly. 'We cannot give
out information on our guests,' he told Cody.
'Especially not that of a lady.'

'I understand.' Cody tried a false smile and said, 'It's
just that her father asked me to look out for her, to be
sure she got to town the way the weather's been.'

The clerk looked thoughtful. His voice was nearly a
whisper when he asked, 'She's not a run away, is she?'

'Nothing like that,' Cody said with what he thought
was a suitable laugh. 'I was coming into town to take
care of some business for her father, and the girl
couldn't wait – she wanted to do some shopping.' Cody
didn't know if his lie was convincing. It probably didn't
matter. What was important was that Lonnie was all
right.

'Tell me, what time does the bank open tomorrow?'

he asked the clerk.

'Precisely at nine o'clock.'

'Tell me, do you have a hotel safe? As I said, I have some business to conduct, and until the bank opens . . .'

'We have a small safe for our residents,' the clerk admitted in a low, cautious voice. Someone else had entered the hotel, and Cody glanced that way at two men he had never seen before, staggering toward their room and speaking in loud voices.

'I hope their room isn't next to mine,' Cody said, and the clerk smiled his understanding.

'No, sir.'

'Then, if you would be good enough to place these in your safe for me...' Cody hoisted the saddle-bags and placed them on the counter. The heavy chinking of the gold coins left little doubt as to what they contained. 'And let me have my room key.'

'Certainly, sir,' the amiable clerk said.

'I'll need a receipt for that, of course,' Cody said.

'Of course, sir,' the man replied as if slightly wounded by the remark. He hefted the heavy saddle-bags and went away to a back room for a few minutes. Cody heard the clang of a heavy steel door closing, then the clerk returned. He filled out a receipt on pink paper and gave it to Cody, who tucked it into his pocket after glancing at it.

A brass door key was passed across the counter. 'Will you require a bath, sir?' the clerk asked.

'I could use one, but not tonight. It's late. In the morning, I suppose, if you can send someone up around eight o'clock. I do have to get to the bank early. For tonight – tell me, could you have some sandwiches brought to my room?'

'I could, sir,' the clerk answered, 'but there is a very fine restaurant attached to the hotel.' He lifted a pointing finger. 'Just through the door over there.'

'All right. That sounds even better. I'll just have a look at my room first.'

Cody made his way upstairs, found his room and entered. The iron bed was neatly made, a burnt-orange coverlet thrown over it. Matching curtains framed a small window which Cody opened a crack to air out the room. A gust of the frigid air forced its way through the gap. Cody smiled. At least he wouldn't be sleeping on the prairie this night.

*As Charlie would be.* He shook that thought out of his mind, shed his scuffed leather coat and placed his rifle in the narrow corner closet. He could ignore his hunger no longer, so he made his way back down the stairs and across the lobby to where the door to the hotel restaurant stood.

He entered a pleasant room with round tables covered with white cloths. It was a warm and fragrant room. Men and ladies sat at their tables, most in town clothes. There were a few trailsmen and local cowhands, who had been stranded by the storm, at the tables along the far wall, near the kitchen, drinking coffee.

He spotted Lonnie across the room, sitting alone. There was something different about her, and as he walked toward her, he figured it out: her hair was brushed to a gloss and pinned up on her head. It

132

changed her looks dramatically. She glanced up with curious eyes as he approached and seated himself without having been invited, and smiled.

'Hope you don't mind me sharing your table,' he said.

'Not at all. Who else is going to share with me? I don't know anyone here. I was just sitting with my coffee, looking at the fine dresses the ladies in this town have on.'

'Well, I'm glad you took my advice,' Cody said. 'You'll be happier here. Aren't you going to eat, Lonnie?'

'I already have,' she said with a satisfied smile. 'When that lady came over. . . .'

'The waitress.'

'Yes. When she came over and told me what they had for dinner, I confessed that I wished it was morning so I could have a good breakfast. Well, she just smiled and said they could make that. Can you imagine, having breakfast at this time of night!'

'Town living does have its advantages,' Cody told her.

'They have fresh eggs! We haven't any chickens at home, you know. The toast was warm from the oven.' She leaned nearer across the table. 'And they had honey for it. Oh, and bacon. We don't have a smoke-house at home either; it was a rare treat.'

'And you had the time to fix your hair,' Cody noted with approval.

'Well,' she said with the excitement of new experiences in her eyes, 'when I got up to my room a woman came in.'

'A maid?'

'If that's what they call them,' Lonnie said, waving an impatient hand. 'She asked me did I want my dress sponged to get rid of the trail dust, and pressed. Imagine – they'll do that for you! So while I was taking my dress off to have it cleaned, this woman also said they had a girl who would wash my hair and comb it out for seventy-five cents. Well, Cody, I told her I didn't want nobody washing my hair but me. So she says how about brushing it and pinning it up for fifty cents.

'And they did!' Lonnie finished, amazed still at the city ways.

'Well, it looks fine,' Cody said honestly. The waitress had approached their table and Cody ordered the special supper, which was pork roast, mashed potatoes and gravy, corn on the cob and apple pie.

'That sounded so good,' Lonnie said when the waitress had gone, 'that if I could possibly do it, I'd eat again myself.'

Cody smiled in return. He could put it off no longer, so he broached the subject. 'Lonnie, we're going to have to talk about the money I have, and Uncle Morris's fortune, again. They seem to be one and the same.'

'Of course they are. That's what I was telling you.'

'Did Uncle Morris tell you how much the fortune was, or where he got it?'

'No.' Lonnie shook her head. 'But a fortune is enough for a person to live on, isn't it? That's what Uncle Morris told me – I could live on it and never have to rely on Emil Stanton again. As to where he got it, we didn't talk that much. He was in a hurry to get me out of there, as I told you.'

'He thought that the man he got it from would come back; and he did.' Cody sighed, moved his arms so that his food could be served, and then told Lonnie, 'Uncle Morris won the money in a card game. There was almost four thousand gold dollars.'

'Well, then?' Lonnie asked. 'If you gamble and win, it's the other fellow's loss. If Uncle Morris won it honestly, it was his money. And he promised it to me. It all seems straightforward to me.'

'It wasn't the man's money to gamble with. It belonged to someone else.'

'Who?'

'Triangle,' Cody said and Lonnie's face tightened.

'Of course it did! Triangle owns everything, doesn't it?' she said bitterly.

'Lonnie, the man gambled away a payroll that belonged to Triangle.'

'What man?' she asked.

'Ned Pierce. He had sold a herd of cattle to the army and was supposed to return with the money. He did not.'

'If he lost it, he's the man who should pay it back,' Lonnie believed. 'Not the man who won it from him in an honest game.'

'Maybe,' Cody said, cutting a bite from the thick slice of pork roast he had been served. Honestly, Cody was not sure himself; it was a matter which required some more thought. He decided to tell Lonnie the entire story of how he had come by the gold as he ate, not leaving out any unpleasant detail.

'You've been through a lot,' Lonnie said when he was finished talking, and had nearly finished with his meal. 'So what are you going to do now?'

'I don't honestly know. Wayne and Charlie were both counting on that money so they could retire comfortably, give up ranching for good and all. Me,' he shrugged, 'I don't mind the work.'

'Except you don't have a job now,' Lonnie pointed out, 'and you certainly can never go back to Triangle.'

'No. But doesn't Jewel Frazier deserve something out of this as well? She wants off the ranch badly.'

'She's a rich girl!' Lonnie complained.

'That doesn't mean she doesn't deserve it. It was her money, after all. Money the Triangle earned.'

'Well, give it to her!' Lonnie said, half-rising from her chair with anger. 'I'll go on home. Amos and Daltry will be happy to see me. It will give them something to peep at again!'

'Lonnie,' Cody pleaded, 'sit down and listen to me.' He tried to keep his voice calm, to calm her. 'What I had in mind was trying to be fair. Just this: suppose I gave Jewel Frazier half of the money? That would be enough for her to do what she has planned. The other half you and I could split. That would be enough to get us both started on our way. Until you could find work, until I can find another job.'

'So Jewel Frazier ends up with twice what I get,' Lonnie said in a very cool voice. Her hands were folded together under her chin.

136

'I don't know!' Cody said in frustration. 'It's just a thought I had, trying to be fair and make everybody happy, when no one will be no matter what I decide. It's something we have to talk about further – and this is not the time or the place,' he added as people started to filter out of the restaurant and the waitress hovered to collect his empty plates. 'Another time, please. Meanwhile, just enjoy Baxter and whatever it has to offer.'

He walked around the table and held her chair for her as she rose. 'Cody,' she said apologetically as they started for the door, 'I'm sorry. I know you really are trying to do what's right.'

'We'll talk later,' Cody said, opening the door for her. The conversation was wearing him out. The impulse to recover the gold from the hotel safe and just hand it over to Lonnie was strong; however, that wasn't the way to go about things. Impulses could lead to deep regrets.

He escorted Lonnie to her room, turned away and walked to his own room as she watched him from the doorway.

He found the door open. Had he locked it? He was not used to using keys on doors and probably had just forgotten. He stepped into the dark room, walked to where the lamp rested on the side table and struck a match, touching it to the flat wick.

The window he had opened earlier to air out the room, he noticed by the lamp's feeble, flickering glow, was now closed. Frowning, Cody turned around slowly, feeling a bit of the storm's icy chill creep up his spine.

137

The man standing in the corner of the room had his revolver drawn and aimed at Cody Hawk.

# ELEVEN

Cody looked at the cold-eyed man who stood in his room, his pistol trained on Cody.

'I guess you've got a reason for being here,' Cody said evenly.

'I guess I do. It's called gold.'

The man waved Cody to his bed, where he sat while the stranger sat in the wooden chair opposite him, one leg crossed over the other, his Colt revolver still in his hand.

'You've got something I want,' the stranger said. He kept his hat on, kept his hand firmly on his pistol. 'I think you know what it is, so don't play the fool.'

'Why me?' Cody asked. 'I can't possibly have anything of yours. I've never seen you before. Who are you?'

'My name,' the intruder said, leaning back slightly in the wooden chair, 'is Billy Post – ever hear the name before?'

'I don't think so . . .' and then Cody believed that he *had* heard the name. Wasn't Billy Post the name of the wrangler who had been riding back to Triangle with Ned Pierce to deliver the army's payment for the steers Triangle had driven up there?

'I see you have,' Post said. He had a rough, somehow crooked face and a sharp chin heavy with trail-stubble.

'I don't know what you want,' Cody Hawk said, glancing toward the partly open door as a pair of drunk men, probably the two he had seen in the lobby earlier, passed noisily by. When they were gone, their voices quieted by the slamming of their room door, Cody said, 'If you're who I think you are you should be talking to Ned Pierce or Frazier, not me. What have I got to do with it?'

'Everything that matters. There's no point in me talking to Ned Pierce. I'd kill him before he got a word out. As for Frazier, he has nothing to do with it. You're the one who has the money, Tucker.'

'I'm not Wayne Tucker.'

'That's the name you signed in the hotel register,' Post said with a sly glint in his hard eyes. 'I looked in the book, trying to find who the last man in was. The man who'd just trailed in from Triangle. I've been trailing you a long way, friend.'

'Since Rios Canyon?' Cody asked, remembering the mysterious man who had been dogging their trail the whole way.

Billy Post nodded. 'Since you left the cabin, Tucker, or whatever your name is.'

'Hawk. Cody Hawk.'

'Since then, Mr Hawk. Because you have something I want. Something I've paid well for these last two years.'

'It's Triangle money,' Cody protested.

140

'Then why didn't you give it to them? Because you're a thief. I think all men are thieves. Some of them just deny it because they've never found themselves in a prime position to help themselves out.'

'I think you're wrong about that,' Cody said. 'What I want to know is this – what makes you think you have any claim to that money? And where have you been for two years?'

'Do you really want to know?' Post asked, his mouth tightening, 'All right, I'll tell you. You remember that army post that used to be up along the Saginaw River? We drove a herd up there to keep the boys alive over the winter. It was tough work, I can tell you, through hard weather and over rough terrain. Ned Pierce was giving the boys hell constantly for things that could not be helped.

'When we were paid, most of the men took their pay and drifted off, saying they'd never work for Triangle under Pierce again. Me, I had a steady job and I got along with Pierce well enough. I stuck with him. We stopped over in McCormack for a rest, you know the town?'

'I do. I used to ride for Domino.'

'Ned got to drinking pretty heavily. He always did like his whiskey, but this was real heavy drinking. Maybe he was thinking about how he was going to tell Ernest Frazier that nearly his entire crew had quit on him. And I guess he started seeing some woman, too. And gambling a lot. I tried to talk to him, saying we ought to be hitting Long Pass before heavy snow started falling.'

141

'He wouldn't listen, of course,' Cody said, knowing Ned Pierce.

'No. One night I was asleep in our hotel room and something woke me. I saw Pierce kneeling on the floor. He had taken the saddle-bags with the money from the cattle sale from under his bed and opened it. I asked him what he was doing and he told me to shut up. He was drunk, of course.

'It seems he had gotten into an all-night card game and he was down on his cash. He was going to borrow some Triangle money to catch up. Of course he never did.'

'He lost about two hundred dollars more that weren't his,' Cody said.

'How did you know?' Billy Post asked.

Everyone kept referring to the missing amount as $4,000, yet when Wayne had counted it at the cabin, there was exactly $3,800. The other $200 Pierce had gambled away in McCormack. Now Pierce would have to explain not only how he had alienated the entire trail crew but lost a part of the money gambling. He would have been feeling the pinch.

'Just a guess. How did you get Pierce out of McCormack?'

'Practically dragged him,' Post answered. 'He was determined to win the money back. Said Frazier would skin him alive.' Cody nodded. From what he had heard about Ernest Frazier before he had gotten ill, he had been a real heller.

'But you got him started down Long Cut before the heavy snows hit?'

142

'We started down, yeah, but the storm just kept building. Pierce was brooding all the way, He was mad at me, the men he had gambled with, afraid of Ernest Frazier. And he didn't like riding sober.

'We camped out one night in the snow, huddled near a small campfire. Pierce looked at me across the fire and said, "I could tell them that we got hit by bandits and they took the money." Of course, that wouldn't do, would it? Why would any bandits take just part of the money? Then I began to see what Pierce had in mind. He meant to take it all and return with his tale.

'He was inviting me in, of course, but I couldn't do it. I wanted to stay on at Triangle and didn't think I could stick to a lie facing Frazier. I didn't answer Ned.

'The next day, in the thick of the storm, he halted his horse and I rode alongside and stopped.

'"I've got to save myself, Billy," Ned Pierce said. "I mean to marry Jewel and take over Triangle one day. I can't let Frazier know what's happened. Are you with me, or not?"

'I told him I couldn't get involved in his scheme,' Billy Post told Cody. 'So without another word he shot me from my horse. He shot me four times and left me for dead on that mountain.'

Cody Hawk shut his eyes tightly for a moment and shook his head. He knew that Pierce was dangerous, but had not realized just how cruel the man was. Billy Post went on:

'I couldn't rise; I couldn't move. The snow kept falling. Every part of my body hurt. He had gotten me

143

in the chest, in both legs and my right shoulder. I don't know how long I lay there, my blood staining the snow. I couldn't describe that day to anybody who would understand. I know what the word agony means now.'

'How'd you survive?' Cody asked, for Billy Post had fallen into a silent, gloomy reverie that lasted many long, dark minutes while lantern-light flickered weirdly on the walls. All this time Cody had been trying to figure a way to reach his pistol, which was hanging in its holster on one of the iron bedposts. He knew that Post had not come here only to unburden his heart. Cody eased over that way and Post came fully alert again and answered him.

'The rarest of chances. An army patrol was cutting up the Long Pass on their way back to the Saginaw post. They picked me and took me back with them. None of them thought I would make it. The post surgeon was a regular doctor, not one of these saw-and-pill docs you find in these remote places. But he just bandaged me up and put me to bed, that was all.

'It was a while before things were explained to me. I needed a lot of surgery and he couldn't be wasting all that time on a civilian while he had other work to do. I had to be a soldier to get that kind of attention.

'Well, Cody Hawk,' Post said with a short laugh, 'those were my choices – enlist or die. Which would you choose? The commander swore me in for a two-year hitch in the US Army, then told the doctor he could start cutting.

'I was a long time abed that winter, a long time healing. A long time hating. As soon as I got to my feet

I started thinking about desertion, but I knew I wasn't strong enough to make it. And I didn't like the idea of facing a firing squad if I got caught.

'Come spring we got the word that the post was being abandoned and we were all going to Montana. I went along, resigned now to just doing my two-year enlistment. Pierce would still be there for the killing when I got out.

'When eventually I was discharged, I started looking in McCormack town, but no one had seen Pierce. Why would he be up there? The army post had been abandoned and they no longer needed cattle. If Pierce wanted to gamble, he would ride to Baxter. I decided to try Triangle first, of course. Now I was risking being lynched by angry cowboys if I killed Pierce instead of having the army firing squad end my life, but my anger remained strong enough to make me reckless.'

'Why follow us if it was Pierce you wanted?'

'A funny thing happened, Cody Hawk. I came across tracks in the snow and was curious. I followed them back to a trapper's shack. I knew that was what it was by the frozen hides I found there. There was still smoke in the fireplace, though the fire was nearly dead. And on the fire was a pair of saddle-bags. I fished them out with the poker and stamped out the flames. They were empty, of course, but I flipped one of the bags over and there were the initials "N.P." burned into the leather.

'That got me to thinking. Then I saw something that looked like a skeleton hand in the corner under the old hides. I flipped the hides aside and saw that this particular dead man had been a card player, and that he had been dead long enough for the flesh to disappear from his bones. Say two years at the least.

'I didn't know what had happened, but if the dead man was not Ned Pierce, then Pierce had killed him. Somehow I didn't think it was Ned lying there. It seemed more likely that Ned had killed someone over the missing money. I went outside and stood there watching the sun glitter on the snow-bound trees and decided that it might be to my benefit to follow whoever had been in that cabin trying to burn Ned's saddle-bags.'

'What did you learn?' Cody asked.

'Not a lot at first. But you were riding in the direction I intended to go anyway, so I tagged along.'

'I need to know,' Cody said, his face now nearly as grim as Billy Post's, 'was it you who killed my friend, Wayne Tucker, back on the Stanton place? Was it you who shot Charlie Tuttle on our way to Baxter?'

'Does it make a difference?' Post asked. Cody thought he again saw movement out in the hallway through the partly opened door, but he ignored it and answered Post.

'Yes, it does. To me.'

Post stifled a crooked grin. He needed Cody's cooperation if it could be had. His answer was succinct.

'If I did shoot them I wouldn't admit it,' the man said with a sly expression.

'If I shot you, I'd admit it and be proud of it,' the voice at the door said. Cody first saw the threatening muzzle of a Winchester rifle intrude into the room, and then Lonnie Stanton entered on bare feet, her hair now let down, her cocked rifle to her shoulder. 'Throw away that pistol or I'll take your head off.'

Billy Post hesitated for only a second before letting his revolver clatter to the floor. He said, 'I believe that you would. I know who you are – you're that wild mountain girl.'

'That's right,' Lonnie replied, 'and Cody Hawk is my friend. I think you'd better get out of here, mister.'

'I think you're right,' Billy Post said, eyeing the small woman and the big Winchester in her hands. 'I'll just pick up my pistol and be on my way.'

'Leave it. You won't be needing it,' Cody said.

Billy Post sneered at him. 'I can get another,' he said.

'You won't be needing that one either. Why don't you just clear out, Post? We won't be doing any business together.'

'We could have you arrested,' Lonnie told the ex-soldier.

'Sure you could,' Post said mockingly. 'But they'd have a lot of questions they'd want answers to. You'd tell your side of the story; I'd tell mine. Then while they figured it out, they'd seize the gold as evidence and tuck it away so that no one could get to it.

'I don't think you want to go to the law, either of you. I can see this isn't the time for talking. I'll be back another time.' He paused. 'With a new pistol.'

'I'll be wearing mine next time,' Cody said.

Post looked Cody up and down. 'I don't think you'd have a chance, cowboy, without your little watchdog here.'

Then Post walked out of the room, smirking.

Lonnie said: 'I almost wish I had shot him.'

'I know, but that wouldn't have done us any good, would it? We'll just have to figure out some other way to get rid of him.'

Lonnie looked doubtful, weary. She sat down on the chair that Post had just vacated and asked Cody quite seriously, 'Do you want me to spend the night here to watch out for you? You're dead tired, Cody, I can tell.'

'No. You've got your own room and your own bed. I will be sleeping with my Colt near at hand on this night, though. If Billy Post could find us, others can too.'

'Ned Pierce, do you mean?'

'Him and your brothers,' Cody replied, bending stiffly to pick up the revolver Post had dropped.

'They're not my brothers except in name,' Lonnie objected, 'but yes, Amos and Daltry could mean trouble if they found us. Except that I don't think they will. They're far too lazy to walk all this way through the snow.'

'Weren't they speaking of trying to steal some Triangle horses from the outriders?'

'Oh, they were always coming up with grand plans,' Lonnie said dismissively. 'Once I heard them sitting around the table discussing how to rob a train, although there is no railroad within a hundred miles.'

'Lonnie?' Cody asked seriously as he lowered himself onto the bed with some difficulty. 'Did they know about Uncle Morris's fortune?'

Lonnie looked at the floor and then up again,

148

apologetically. 'I thought I told you. Uncle Morris told me to never say a word, but one night I was so angry with them, with everyone, that I blurted something out about how I would be leaving soon because Uncle Morris was going to give me some money, a lot of money.'

'Did they believe you?'

'Enough so that Amos and Daltry traipsed up to Long Pass and visited the cabin. They said they searched everywhere but there was no money hidden in Uncle Morris's shack. They came back madder than anything. They told me I'd sent them on a wild goose chase.'

Cody nodded thoughtfully. 'Did they tell you Uncle Morris was dead? If they searched the entire cabin, they must have found his body.'

'They told me,' Lonnie said, 'and I cried myself to sleep that night and for many nights afterwards, because I knew that Uncle Morris was gone and that he had taken my dreams with him.'

'Then they no longer believe in the fortune?'

'I don't think so. Not enough to come all the way to Baxter chasing after it.'

'What about you, Lonnie?' Cody asked. 'Would they come all this way for you? To take you back?'

Lonnie laughed lightly, sadly. 'Why? I'm just one more mouth to feed to the Stanton clan.'

Cody nodded, figuring that that was probably so. Their immediate problem, then, was getting rid of Billy Post and hoping that Ned Pierce – who knew that the fortune was no myth – wasn't looking for them.

'I can't think straight any more, Lonnie. I've got to get some rest.' He moved his injured leg carefully onto the bed.

'How bad is it?' Lonnie wanted to know. She couldn't help but notice the way Cody had been favoring his leg.

'Not bad,' he answered, pulling his boots off. She could see the tight bandaging around his ankle and winced with sympathy.

'Sprained, is it?'

'Or broken. No one could be sure,' Cody answered with what he hoped was a cheerful smile. 'But it doesn't bother me so much as my knee. It locks up from time to time.'

'Let me have a look at it,' Lonnie said, rising.

'Let you what?'

'Oh, for God's sake, Cody, I have seen a man's leg before! I want to see if I can do anything for you.'

She was serious and quite firm. So was Cody when he answered. 'Not now. I don't want a woman looking at my leg. Go on back to your room and get a good night's sleep. I intend to try to do the same.'

The look in her eyes was slightly hurt. Cody knew that many women were nurses by nature, but that didn't mean he wanted this one probing, poking and commenting on his torn knee. Lonnie nodded and, with that hurt expression still on her face, she went out of the room, closing the door firmly. Following her that way, limping as he went, Cody inserted the key and locked it. Then he rolled into bed, and with his Colt under his pillow he closed his eyes, trying not to think about what further trouble morning might bring.

It shouldn't have been a surprise, but it was.

Walking stiffly to his window to greet the new morning, Cody saw a town heavy with snow, few people yet moving around to disturb the even blanket along the main street of Baxter. But there, opposite his window, standing on the plankwalk, gazing up at the hotel, stood Jewel Frazier.

She wore a fur-collared green jacket and matching green skirt. Her hands were concealed in a heavy fur muff. If she was there, could Ned Pierce be far away?

Cody cursed softly and began to dress. Today was the day that it was all to end one way or the other. The chill along his spine was still there: a cold, warning tingle as if the skeleton himself had finally come to collect his dues.

# TWELVE

There was sharp, urgent rapping at the hotel room door as Cody finished dressing, holstering his Colt and buckling his gunbelt. He opened the door cautiously to find Lonnie, her hair still down but knotted back in some fashion, looking up at him with startled eyes. It was so unusual to see the mountain girl with anything like fear in her expression that Cody frowned, opened the door and allowed her to slip quickly into the room.

'You'll never guess who I just saw,' Lonnie said breathlessly. Cody thought that he could guess, nevertheless he asked:

'Who?'

'That Ned Pierce from Triangle. He was down in the lobby.'

Cody answered slowly, uncertainly. 'We have to get to the bank. Be there as soon as it opens., Once the money is locked away there, they'll have no reason to keep hounding us.'

'But . . .'

But getting there was going to be the tricky part.

First things first. 'Let's go down to the desk. I've got to claim my saddle-bags.'

'He'll be waiting for us outside. He's a murderous man, Cody,' Lonnie said with glistening eyes. 'I know that.'

'No matter. The sooner we move, the better. We can't hole up in the hotel and hope they don't find us – they undoubtedly already know we're here.'

'You keep saying "they".'

'Jewel Frazier has come along with him. If you look out my window you may still be able to see her across the street. She's wearing green.'

'Her!' Lonnie said disparagingly. 'I'm not afraid of her.'

'She does carry a pistol,' Cody warned her, remembering the little nickel-plated revolver Jewel had brandished in her house. 'In her skirt pocket, or maybe tucked inside the muff she's carrying.'

'I'll bet she's never had to face down anything like my Winchester,' Lonnie said. 'Let me go back to my room and get it. I'll show her something.'

'That's not a good idea,' Cody said. 'Town women don't go marching down the street with their rifles. You'll just draw more attention to us. I'm armed and I've asked: it's only three blocks to the bank.'

'Your Colt may not be enough,' Lonnie protested, and in that she was right, but neither did they want to ignite a full-blown gunfight in the streets of Baxter. The local law would be drawn in immediately, and they did not need to have men with badges involved in this – Billy Post had been correct about that.

'It's better this way,' Cody said uncertainly. He thought that the sight of the little mountain girl with a Winchester rifle traipsing down the street guarding a man with heavy saddle-bags over his shoulder might set people to wondering. He would just have to try his luck with Billy Post and Ned Pierce if it came to that. Both were known gunmen and Cody had never shot a man in his life.

Having to do so now would have the opposite effect to what he wanted – to move the gold quietly to the bank, where it would be secure and be available for Lonnie to live on for as long as she needed it. He admitted it to himself now – it was hers. It was Uncle Morris's last bequest. If anyone had a right to the skeleton's gold it was Lonnie Stanton. At least, she was the only one with a claim to it who didn't seem ready to kill him for it.

The desk clerk was a different man from the one who had checked them in. Rounder, shorter, with thin red hair. He was just as affable, however; a trait that seemed to be desirable for men in such positions. Cody gave him his claim check, which the clerk muttered over, smiled and muttered some more, before retreating to the back office and returning with Cody's saddle-bags. Lonnie stood by watching nervously, her eyes switching from point to point, surveying the hotel lobby. She seemed not to know what to do with her hands without her rifle.

Cody did not open the saddle-bags to check their contents. He asked, 'Is there a back door we could use?'

'There is one in the inner office, sir. Why. . . ?' He did not finish the question. These men were of a discreet breed. He offered to direct them through since there were no other waiting guests. Passing through the small, yellow-painted room, Cody noticed a brass-bound clock on the wall. It read ten minutes to nine.

'Is that clock right?' Cody asked. The man looked briefly offended by the question.

'Of course,' he replied, his manner a little stuffy. The clerk opened the back door with some difficulty. There was snow piled up outside in the back alley. The reflected morning sun was brilliant. A gust of cold wind blew in. Cody glanced outside, back to Lonnie and stepped out, his boots crunching through the crust on top of the newly fallen snow. Lonnie followed, pausing to shiver and wrap her arms around herself. She wore no jacket. They had left hurriedly.

'How far?' she asked, her lips trembling just a little.

'Just three blocks; I told you. I'm sorry about dragging you out, but it was time to go.'

'It's all right,' she said, still shivering. The sky was blue, dotted with sparse clouds beyond a long line of leafless gray willow trees. A fitful breeze shuffled the branches of the trees. There were distant human sounds across town, but they saw no one. Along the alley there were only the tracks of a single man's boots accompanied by a dog's footprints in the snow.

Cody had the heavy saddle-bags slung over his shoulder. He had folded back the flap of his old leather jacket to allow access to his revolver. He strode so quickly along the snowy alleyway that Lonnie had to

155

break into a trot to keep up with him. They were too close to the end to grow careless or slow down now.

'We'll make it,' Cody said encouragingly to Lonnie after another block. Her breath steamed out as she spoke an unheard word and nodded. Her eyes were hopeful and uncertain at once.

That was when Ned Pierce stepped out from a cross-alley, his big blue pistol in his hand, coat collar tugged up around his jawline, hat tugged low, expression grim and menacing.

'I believe you've got something that belongs to me, Cody Hawk.'

'No. I don't,' Cody said, halting, shifting his feet slightly to ready himself for a draw. Though what chance he had against an experienced shooter who already had the drop on him was beyond minimal.

Pierce was smiling coldly. 'Let's not make this any worse, Cody Hawk,' he said. 'Just drop those saddle-bags and I'll let you walk away.'

The alley was empty. Cody had forced Lonnie to leave her rifle behind for her own protection. He regretted that now. Pierce drew back the hammer of his Colt .44. 'I've no grudge against you, Hawk. All I want is the money.'

'That's all you ever cared about, isn't it, Ned?' a wild voice asked from out of the cross-alley. Cody shifted his eyes that way. He could see only the man's arm and the pistol it held, but he recognized the voice of Billy Post.

'Post?' Ned Pierce said in obvious confusion. 'How did you ever get here? If you think I owe you something, we can work it out.' Pierce's voice was uncertain, tinged with something near panic.

'Oh, you owe me something, Ned,' Post said, taking another step forward from the alley. 'Like two years of my life, six months of it spent in a hospital bed. How much do you figure that's worth, Ned?'

'I didn't mean for it to happen,' Ned tried weakly. Billy Post didn't let him get further with his denial.

'I know,' Post said with heavy sarcasm. 'You shot me four times accidentally and then left me in the mountains to freeze to death, to bleed to death, but you didn't mean to do it.'

Ned Pierce was quaking now. He could hear the rage in Post's words. Pierce tried again: 'Billy, take the money. I guess I owe you that. But there's no point in killing me. Not over old quarrels.'

'That's what you call it?' Billy Post erupted. It was obvious he meant to shoot, to kill Pierce. 'I'll have the money, all right, and I'll have my revenge!'

Cody pulled Lonnie behind him to shield her. Post's .44 exploded in the stillness of the snowy morning. Cody saw Pierce take a bullet full in the chest and stagger back. As he tried to level his own aim, his knee buckled and he went down to lie sprawled in the snow. Post took three steps forward and hovered over the Triangle foreman as he twitched, breathed his last and died. There was a maniacal gleam in Post's eyes as he shifted them toward Cody and Lonnie Stanton.

'Now then!' Billy Post roared. 'How are you going to play it, cowboy?'

Before Cody could frame any sort of answer, a wild banshee cry rose from the alleyway and Jewel Frazier burst from it, screaming and wailing at once. She looked once at Cody and Lonnie, then pulled that small nickel-plated pistol from her fur muff and shot Billy Post, who was too astonished to react as the bullet struck him in the face, producing a bloody mask. He was already dead, but his reflexes were not. A tremor of his finger against the trigger of his Colt caused it to erupt with smoke and flame and the onrushing Jewel Frazier took a bullet in her breast, waved her arms like windmills, and her lovely face plowed into the snow a few feet from her dead foreman.

Lonnie gripped Cody's arm tightly. Her voice was tremulous. 'Cody, we have to—'

'We have to get out of here,' Cody said, taking her hand and yanking her along after him. The shots would draw a crowd. They reached the main street as a man with a silver shield was rushing toward them, hatless, hair in disarray. Cody didn't wait for the questions. He pointed and said, 'Some sort of ruckus back there, Marshal.'

The lawman hurried along. Lonnie leaned her head against Cody's shoulder in relief and they walked on toward the bank. People up and down the street were rushing toward the alley where the triple killing had taken place. Lonnie was shaking; Cody wasn't much steadier. They reached the bank door just as a small man in a blue town suit was unlocking the front door with the key he kept on a gold chain.

'Something going on?' he asked.

'Some sort of gunfight,' Cody said and the banker nodded his head. So long as it did not constitute a

threat to his bank, it did not concern him.

'Well,' Cody said as he and Lonnie sat together in the cool sunshine on a bench on front of the hotel, 'it's done. You're a rich girl now.' They had split the money fifty-fifty, realizing that there was no one else left alive who had any claim to it, and had opened matching bank accounts.

'Is that enough money to feel rich on, Cody? To tell you the truth, I don't feel rich – and I sure wouldn't go through that all again to make some money!'

'No. Well – at least you're better off than you were before.'

'I was thinking,' Lonnie said after a pause, 'that I might try to find work in the hotel. That's the most elegant place I've ever seen.'

'You could try it, I suppose,' Cody answered, watching a trio of cowhands ride past, churning up the snow, 'but you've plenty of money to last you for a few years. You ought to try first to find a place of your own. A small house. Nothing is more elegant than your own home.'

'Is that true?' she asked, looking up with liquid eyes. Her hands were folded together between her knees.

'So they tell me,' Cody answered. 'I've never had my own home, so I don't really know.'

'You've got enough money now to find a small cottage for yourself, Cody Hawk.'

'I suppose I do,' Cody said, breathing in deeply, 'but then what would I do for a living?'

'What will I do? What does anyone do, Cody?'

Lonnie said, with eagerness now showing in her eyes. 'Your leg will heal by spring. You can do whatever you want. Right now you have no job, no prospects. You might as well settle in Baxter while the snow is falling. We'll be neighbors!' she said with girlish good cheer.

Cody was less enthusiastic, but what Lonnie said was true enough – where was he to go, how was he to work over the winter, the shape he was in, the weather as it was?

'Or,' the girl said with still more enthusiasm, 'we could share a house! That way it would only cost us half as much. It would stretch out our fortunes.'

Cody moved uneasily on the wooden bench. 'I'm not sure that's such a great idea, Lonnie.'

'Well, sure it is,' she said, standing. There was a bright smile on her lips. 'That way I could look after your leg, and you could look after mine!'

'Why, what's the matter with your legs?' Cody asked uncertainly. Then he caught the meaning of Lonnie's smile and looked away toward the hotel restaurant.

'I wonder what they're fixing for dinner?'

He rose and started toward the hotel door with Lonnie not far behind him. He thought that things might be that way for a long time to come.